Something's
BREWING

Something's BREWING

Short Stories & Plays for Everyone

Jillian Ober & Tom Fish

proving press

Book Design & Production:
Columbus Publishing Lab
www.ColumbusPublishingLab.com

Copyright © 2020 by
Jillian Ober and Tom Fish
LCCN: 2020919526

Paperback ISBN: 978-1-63337-463-8
E-Book ISBN: 978-1-63337-438-6

Printed in the United States of America
1 3 5 7 9 10 8 6 4 2

Acknowledgments

THIS BOOK WOULD NOT HAVE BEEN POSSIBLE without the generous support of Mr. Robert Woodward and the GLOW Foundation. Their support enabled us to publish this book and use its proceeds to support Next Chapter Book Club operations worldwide. We are honored to know such a tremendous family!

We are thankful to talented photographer Sebastian Popescu for most of the images you'll see in this book. We're also very grateful to the Next Chapter Book Club members, volunteers and friends who served as photo models to help us bring these stories and plays to life.

Big thank-you hugs to our longtime friends and colleagues, Dr. Paula Rabidoux and Dr. Anke Gross-Kunkel, for generously agreeing to review the manuscript.

We also express deep gratitude to our editor and publisher, Emily Hitchcock. She is cool, calm and collected and certainly makes our work shine.

Lastly, writing a book together is not always easy. So, we want to thank one another for a lot of cooperation and respect.

Foreword

THIS BOOK IS ABOUT SIX PEOPLE who belong to the same Next Chapter Book Club (NCBC). Each of the first six short stories features one of the main characters who tells us a story in their own words. Following the stories are six plays that involve these characters, their book club facilitators, and various other people. Even though the characters and events in this book are made up, the book club members have similar successes, challenges, hopes and dreams as real NCBC members.

Next Chapter Book Club is an international program of over 350 book clubs for people with intellectual and developmental disabilities (IDD). Since the beginning of NCBC in 2002, we have continued to find very few books that are *both* accessible *and* age-appropriate for adults with IDD. So, we wrote this book with relatable adult themes and used clear, simple language. The book also features large print, photographs, and guided discussion questions.

While the stories and plays do not focus on the characters' disabilities, they do not shy away from them either. As you read or listen, we hope that you will find a character or situation you can relate to, and in the end, know that you belong.

Have fun reading. Try not to take yourself too seriously, and feel free to laugh out loud along the way.

With affection,

Tom and Jillian

Dedication

This book is dedicated to Emily Savors, who believed in the Next Chapter Book Club from the very beginning, as well as to all the extraordinary NCBC Volunteer Facilitators around the world.

To learn more about Next Chapter Book Club, visit:

www.nextchapterbookclub.org

Story 1

We Need to Talk

I JUST HAD A HECK OF A WEEK! There were so many ups and downs. I'll tell you about it.

First, the Chicago Bears won on Sunday. That's always a good thing! My aunt and uncle came over to watch the game. Everyone wore their Bears shirts and hats. We grilled hamburgers and hot dogs. We cheered and yelled at the TV and had a lot of fun.

Monday was a little boring. But I guess that's a regular Monday. My girlfriend Josie and I work at the same place. That's where we met. It's a big warehouse they call a distribution center. So, even when work is boring, I still get to see my girlfriend.

I asked her to go on a date with me on her very first day at work. Josie (and a few other people) told me that was too soon. I waited one month and asked her out again. She accepted. We have been dating ever since. I really like having a girlfriend.

Tuesday night, I took Josie out to dinner. She just found out that she was getting a new roommate, and she wanted to celebrate. Josie said her first roommate was messy and selfish.

Josie wanted to get sushi for dinner. I think sushi is gross. But since we were celebrating Josie's good news, I let her pick the restaurant. Other than the fact that I didn't like anything on the menu, we had a good time at dinner. The bus I take home was late that night, so I was really tired and still hungry when I got home.

As soon as I walked in the door, my mom handed me a laundry basket full of my dirty clothes.

"You need to wash your clothes, Steve," my mom said. "Do you have any clean clothes left for work?" she asked.

"Yeah, I have a few things," I said. I didn't actually know if I had any clean clothes. But at that moment, I was too hungry to think about laundry. I put the basket on the kitchen floor and started looking for a snack.

"I thought you and Josie just went to dinner. Are you hungry already?" my mom asked.

"Josie wanted to go to the sushi place. There isn't anything I like to eat there," I told my mom.

"Do you see, Steve? This is another example of what your dad and I are talking about. You and Josie seem to do whatever *she* wants. Did you tell her that you didn't want to get sushi for dinner?" my mom asked.

"Yeah, I told her I wanted to go to Burger Barn," I said, "but we were celebrating *her* good news. She's getting a new roommate. She said it was a special occasion. I didn't want to ruin it, so we went to the sushi place. Is all the leftover pizza gone?"

"You mean she will eat raw fish, but she won't eat a burger?" my mom asked.

"She doesn't eat the fish sushi," I explained. My parents think it is silly not to eat meat. "She had the vegetable sushi."

My mom rolled her eyes. I'm not always sure what she means when she does that. But it made me upset, so I said, "Well, *you* don't have to eat it."

"Neither do you, Steve. You should be able to go eat somewhere that you both like." My mom went on, telling me how I was letting Josie boss me around. That just makes me angry. So, I went to my room and turned on the sports channel. A couple minutes later, my dad knocked on my door and opened it.

"Steve," he said, "I almost tripped over the basket of dirty clothes you left on the kitchen floor. Get up and carry it down to the basement, please.

You should probably go ahead and get started on your laundry while you're down there." Now my dad was telling me what to do, too.

Once I carried the basket downstairs, I did not feel like doing laundry. I was still hungry, so I decided to get a snack instead. I made myself a bowl of cereal and took it to my room to eat. I decided I would do laundry another day.

On Wednesday morning, I wished that I had done my laundry the night before. The only clean shirt I could find was an old Bon Jovi concert T-shirt. It was too small, but at least it was clean. I put a sweatshirt over it and headed to work.

I usually stop for coffee on my walk to the bus stop. The place where I get my coffee has a contest with a grand prize of $1,000! I've been trying to win for the past five months, so I've been buying a lot of coffee. On that morning, I pulled the sticker off my cup and won a free cup of coffee! It wasn't the grand prize, but I was still happy about it. Plus, I have a feeling I'm going to win the money soon. My girlfriend Josie thinks the contest is silly and a waste of money. I'm going to keep trying anyway.

Then, there were free donuts in the break room when I got to work. Free coffee *and* free donuts! That's a great way to start a day. I carried my coffee and donut directly to Josie's work station. She was already working. I wanted to let her know that she was wrong about the contest at the coffee shop.

"Guess who won a free coffee this morning," I said.

"Who?" she said.

I held up my coffee cup and gave it a little shake. "I did. I suppose the contest isn't so silly after all, huh?" I wanted Josie to admit she was wrong.

"It's still silly and a waste of your money. Plus, all those disposable cups are really bad for the environment. But, congratulations on the free coffee," she said. She shook her head and smiled at the same time.

It wasn't the reaction I wanted. She still thought the contest was a waste of money. She still thought she was right. I walked back to my work station and drank my free coffee and ate my free donut. They still tasted good. My dad always says that free food is the best food. I think he's right.

It was warm outside, so I took my sweatshirt off on the walk to the bus stop after work. When I got on the bus, a guy at the front of the bus said, "Hey man,

I think I went to that Bon Jovi concert! That was way back in the day!" We talked about our favorite Bon Jovi songs. It was cool to meet another fan of one of my favorite bands.

When I got home, I went down to the basement and started my laundry. When I walked back upstairs in my tight T-shirt, my mom and dad looked at me. Then they started laughing.

"My goodness, Steve. I didn't realize you'd spread out so much in the middle!" my mom said. I looked down and realized my belly was sticking out from under the T-shirt.

"Yeah, I guess my shirt is a little tight," I said.

"A *little*?" my mom said. "Your T-shirt is living on a prayer!" I was surprised my mom knew the words to my favorite Bon Jovi song.

That night, my dad grilled his famous pork chops and my mom made an apple crisp for dessert. There was even vanilla ice cream to put on top. This was a good night.

On my walk to the bus stop Thursday morning, Josie texted me. The text said, "We need to talk." I called her right away, but she didn't answer her phone. Why would she say that we needed to talk, but then not answer her phone? I felt frustrated, and I planned to tell her when I got to work.

Josie was already busy working when I got to my station. I put my jacket down and I walked over to her. "What did you want to talk about?" I asked.

"We can't talk about it here at work, Steve," she said.

"Fine. We'll talk tonight," I said, even though I didn't want to wait all day to find out what Josie wanted to talk about.

"I can't talk tonight either. I'm going to visit my grandma with my dad. We will have to talk after work tomorrow," Josie said.

"Come on, Josie," I said. "You just texted me to say that we need to talk. But now we can't talk until tomorrow? Can you at least tell me what you want to talk about?"

"No, not here at work," she answered. Then she got right back to work. She seemed upset, and I assumed she was upset with me. But I had no idea why. I was starting to feel angry, so I walked away.

Sometimes I have a bad temper. I'm better at handling my temper than I used to be. Once I threw a baseball through the living room window because the Chicago Cubs lost a game in the ninth inning. It took me a while to pay for that window.

The rest of the day was busy, so it went by fast. I was glad about that. I was also looking forward to watching Thursday Night Football with my dad. It turned out to be a really good game. My dad and I stayed up late to watch the Raiders lose in the last minute of the game.

On Friday morning, I stopped for coffee as usual. I didn't win anything. Oh well, I thought. I'll keep trying.

After work, I waited by the door for Josie. Her sister usually picks her up, but I didn't see her car yet. I hoped we would have some time to talk. Then I saw Josie walking toward me. I had been nervous about this conversation since yesterday morning. That made me feel angry with her.

Then I had an idea.

I often felt nervous about upsetting Josie. I did not want to feel that way. I thought I should break up with her. By the time Josie met me at the door, I had made my decision. "Can we talk outside?" I asked.

"Yes, please," she said. "I asked my sister to pick me up ten minutes late so we could talk."

"Good," I said. Then, as we were walking over to a bench, I just blurted it out. "I think we should break up."

"You do? Why?" Josie asked. I could tell she was surprised. I was surprised at myself. She sat down on the bench. I didn't feel like sitting down yet.

I thought about saying some things that weren't nice. I thought about saying that sushi is a stupid food. I thought about saying that I wouldn't share any of the prize money with her when I won the coffee contest.

Instead, I told her it was very rude to make me wonder and worry the past two days about what she wanted to talk about. I told her it made me feel frustrated and upset, and I didn't want to feel that way anymore. So, I decided that we should break up.

"You *just* decided this? You are so impulsive," she said.

"What do you mean by that?" I asked her.

She said that I didn't take enough time to think about my decision. I was about to disagree with her when she said, "It doesn't matter, though. I was going to break up with you anyway."

"What? Why were *you* going to break up with *me*?" I asked.

"I got a new job. I start on Monday. I'm going to be a hostess in a restaurant. My new boss said my hours will be different each week. Since we aren't going to see each other anymore, I thought it would be best to break up," Josie said.

I was about to ask her why we couldn't see each other outside of work when I remembered that I had just broken up with her.

Josie kept talking. "Also, you know we don't have very much in common, Steve. I don't like your temper either," she said.

"I have never lost my temper with you," I said. But at that moment, I felt like I could lose my temper if I wasn't careful. I sat down on the bench.

"I know, but I have seen you lose your temper. Do you remember when you yelled at the guy at the ice cream shop for giving you a cup instead of a cone? Also, I heard you and your mom having a fight on the phone last week. I don't like that, Steve," Josie said. She seemed very calm. I wondered how she could be so calm.

"So, are we broken up now?" I asked.

"Yes. I'm sorry, Steve," she said.

"It's fine. I broke up with you first, remember?" I said. It didn't feel like a nice thing to say, but I didn't care. I felt hurt. "I should probably go," I said.

"Okay, goodbye," Josie said. Her sister had pulled into the parking lot while we were talking. She stood up and walked to the car. Before she got inside, she waved at me.

I waved back and said, "Bye." I stood up and walked in the other direction toward the bus stop.

I had so many thoughts going through my head. Josie was my first girlfriend since high school. I liked having someone to hang out with. It was true that we usually did what she wanted to do. I didn't care too much as long as I wasn't missing any games on TV. Josie always said I cared too much about sports.

I wondered if breaking up with Josie was impulsive, like she had said. I knew I would miss her, even if she was a little bossy. That made me feel sad.

When I got home, my sister Karen's car was in the driveway. That meant she must be home from college for the weekend. I like it when Karen is home. I walked in the door and heard my family talking in the kitchen.

"Hey, there's the man," my sister said. She walked over and gave me a hug. It felt nice, and I hugged her back. "How's it going, brother?" she asked.

"Josie and I broke up," I blurted out.

"Oh, gosh. I'm sorry," she said. She gave me another hug, and this hug felt nice, too. My parents walked over and said things like, "I'm sorry," and, "We are here for you," and, "Maybe this is for the best."

Karen asked me what happened. I told my family about the text Josie sent me yesterday and our conversation today after work.

"Well, son, you know your mom and I didn't think you and Josie were the best fit," my dad said in a really kind voice.

"I know," I said. "I'm still going to miss her."

"Sure you will," my mom said. "I'm proud of you for not losing your temper." My dad and sister said they were proud of me, too. I looked at my family, and I realized that I was proud of myself, too. I knew I would be okay.

• • • • • • • • • •

I still miss Josie sometimes. After all, we spent a lot of time together. Maybe she was bossy, but she was also a good friend to me. I don't want to forget that.

I should also mention that two weeks later, I won a free bagel from the coffee shop contest. The free blueberry bagel tasted so good with my coffee. When I walked into work that morning, I saw a sign about a lunchtime speaker who was going to tell us about a new book club. I ended up joining that book club.

We meet every Wednesday night at a coffee shop that has *really* good coffee. Sometimes, instead of a book, we even read the sports page. This is the group for me.

What Do You Think?

1.   Are you dating anyone now? If not, would you like to be?

2.   Have you ever broken up with someone? Was it an easy or hard thing to do?

3.   Have you ever dated anyone that your family did not like?

4.   Steve had trouble controlling his temper at times. Do you think it is difficult to control your temper? What do you do when you feel upset?

5.   Have you ever tried to win a contest? Did you win anything?

Story 2

Big Jim's Bossy Boss

HAVE YOU EVER BEEN ON A ROLLER COASTER? They go up and down and spin you around. I used to like roller coaster rides. But now, my *life* feels like a roller coaster ride, and I do not like it.

There have been so many changes in the past couple months. Change is hard. My mood has gone up and down like a roller coaster. I have been happy and sad, and confused and frustrated, and even a little dizzy.

One recent change in my life is my new roommate, Emma. My old roommate of six months, Rose, moved out because we did not get along. Rose said I was too bossy. All she had to do was follow the rules of our apartment. But Rose thought there were too many rules. I told her we had to have rules so that things were fair. Well, it did not work out. (The same thing happened with Wendy, my roommate *before* Rose. Wendy only lived with me for two months!)

Now I live with Emma. So far, she seems really nice, even if she does turn up the TV way too loud. Emma's sister Maggie has come over to visit a few times, and she seems really nice, too. Maggie is helping us write new apartment rules. I hope Emma follows the rules. I do not want to change roommates again.

Another really big change in my life was breaking up with my boyfriend Steve a month ago. I made the decision to break up with Steve for a few reasons. First of all, he has trouble controlling his temper sometimes. I don't like that. He never lost his temper with me, but I heard him yell at his mom on the phone a bunch of times. Once when we were getting ice cream, he yelled at the worker, and everyone in the ice cream shop turned and looked at us. I was so embarrassed.

Plus, Steve's parents aren't very nice. Once, Steve's mom called me "bossy" in a text. Steve didn't know that I saw it, but I did. I think I'm helpful, not bossy. I do the right things, and I think other people should, too.

However, the main reason I decided to break up with Steve was because there was one more big change about to happen in my life—a new job. Steve and I met at work, and we would see each other at the warehouse every day. Then, my service coordinator, Julie, helped me find a new job.

This meant I wouldn't see Steve at work every day. Since neither of us drive, breaking up seemed like the right thing to do.

Remember the roller coaster I mentioned? Well, just as I was about to tell Steve that I wanted to break up, he broke up with me! I was really surprised. It's okay, though. We broke up without fighting, which I was glad about. Maybe we could even be friends someday, if we ever see each other again.

Three weeks ago, I started my new job. I'm a hostess at Big Jim's Hilltop Barbecue. It's a little strange working at a barbecue restaurant since I'm a vegetarian. That means I don't eat meat. But Big Jim's has the best macaroni and cheese and lots of other sides I can eat. At Big Jim's, I greet people as they walk in the restaurant. I decide where customers sit and do lots of other things. I was so bored at the warehouse! I did the same thing all day, every day. At Big Jim's, each day is a little different.

On my first day at Big Jim's, I mostly followed another hostess named Shauna as she did her job. Shauna talks very fast. I learned that hostesses and hosts (there is one man named Keith who is a host) do a lot more than just show people to their seats. We also help servers and bussers with their jobs whenever we have time. We wipe down the menus, which get really gross at a barbecue restaurant! We answer the phone, saying, "Thank you for calling Big Jim's Hilltop Barbecue! How can I help you?"

We also restock the toothpicks and mints for customers to take as they are leaving. You wouldn't believe how many mints some people take! You are only supposed to take one mint, but one of our regular customers named Tim fills up his pockets every time he eats at Big Jim's. I was going to tell him that he was taking too many mints, but Shauna said that I shouldn't.

"The customer is always right," Shauna said.

"But what if they are wrong?" I asked.

"We pretend that they are right. It is the best thing to do if you want to keep customers coming to your restaurant. So, we keep restocking the mints because Tim keeps coming back to eat here. Does that make sense?" Shauna asked.

"I guess so. I don't want to make any customers upset. But it isn't right to take all those mints," I said.

During this conversation on my first day at Big Jim's, I met Sadie. My interview was with the other manager, Derek. Derek seemed nice. Sadie did not.

"I suppose it's not *right*, but it isn't our decision to make, is it?" Sadie said. Then she continued, "Hi, I'm Sadie, the general manager at Big Jim's. I overheard your conversation, and wanted to make sure no one is confused about the rules." Sadie introduced herself without offering to shake my hand. I thought that was strange.

"Hi, I'm Josie. Today is my first day," I responded.

"I'm filling Josie in on all the things we do up here in the front of the restaurant," Shauna added.

"Fine, I will let you get back to it," Sadie said. "I have plenty to do to keep the rest of this place running," she said. Sadie waved her arm in the direction of the dining room and kitchen. Then she shook her head, sighed, and walked away.

"*Anyway*," Shauna said, "here's a copy of the table chart. It shows how the restaurant is laid out. Each table is numbered. It will be important for you to memorize this. Big Jim's gets very busy at lunchtime, and having the table numbers memorized will help things go smoothly."

I took the paper and nodded at Shauna. For the first time that day, I felt nervous. Memorizing things like this chart is hard for me. What if I couldn't memorize it fast enough? What if I made a mistake in front of Sadie? That would be the worst.

Shauna tried to help me feel better. She could tell that the chart overwhelmed me. "Just do your best, Josie. You'll know the table numbers in no time," she said with a smile. I appreciated that.

The lunch rush had begun, and for the rest of the day, I followed Shauna and did what I could to help her. The next day, Keith was my trainer. Before lunch, he talked with me about how hosts and hostesses decide where to seat customers.

"It depends on how many servers are working and whose turn it is for a new table. And then sometimes, when we're in the weeds—that's how we say 'busy' here in the restaurant biz—you just do the best you can. Most of the servers understand if they get double-sat or triple-sat," Keith said.

"What does that mean? Double-sat and triple-sat?" I asked. I was starting to feel nervous again.

"Sorry," Keith said. "That's more restaurant lingo. A server is 'double-sat' if we seat customers at two different tables in their section at the same time. If we seat people at *three* open tables in their section at the same time, they are 'triple-sat.' It can be harder for the server to make sure customers get timely service if so many are seated at the same time."

"Okay, I won't do that," I said to Keith.

"Well, sometimes you don't have a choice. If the only three open tables in the restaurant are in Flo's section, then those will be the next three tables that get new customers. It's no biggie if it's Flo, though. She's an old pro," Keith said. "Don't worry, Josie. You'll get the hang of it."

"I hope so," I said. Just then, we heard Sadie's voice from the kitchen.

"Oh, yeah," Keith said, "that's the other thing you should learn. Sadie is the general manager. Did you meet her yesterday?" I nodded and remembered how unfriendly she was.

"You said you interviewed with Derek, right?" I nodded. Keith went on, "He's a nice guy and a good manager. On the other hand, Sadie is...um...tough," he said. Keith was almost whispering to me, and I got the feeling that he was telling me a secret. He looked around us, then said, "Here's the truth. No one likes Sadie here. She's mean for no good reason. But she's the *general* manager, which means she is Derek's boss too," Keith explained.

Keith went on to tell me how grumpy Sadie could be. He said everyone at Big Jim's talks about her. They joke that Big Jim's should be called Big *Sadie's* Hilltop Barbecue because Sadie acts like this is *her* restaurant. He said Sadie is very strict about the rules, even when it doesn't make sense to follow them.

"I'm good at following rules," I told Keith, feeling a little relieved. Maybe if I followed all the rules, which I like to do anyway, I would be okay.

"Well, that's good," Keith said.

A family with three kids walked in. I grabbed three kids' menus and two regular menus. Keith smiled and gave me a thumbs-up. I smiled back. I followed Keith to the table he chose for them.

When we walked back to the front of the restaurant, Sadie was there.

"Great. More kids," Sadie said, like she wasn't happy at all about the kids. "Jodie, after you see the kinds of messes kids leave behind, you'll know why I gave the bussers extra cleaning duties."

"My name is Josie," I told Sadie.

"Sorry, *Josie*," Sadie said my name really loud. I wondered if I should have just let her call me Jodie. "Anyway, it looks like the lunch rush is about to start," she said.

After she walked away, I asked Keith, "Does Big Jim ever come into the restaurant?"

"I wish," he answered. "Jim retired and moved to Tampa, Florida, two years ago. He never said much when he was here, but he seemed like a nice guy. Sadie didn't act like this when he was here either. And here are some more customers walking in," Keith said, and the lunch rush began.

Over the next few weeks, I learned all the table numbers with help from Keith, Shauna, and Shauna's girlfriend, Kelly. Kelly likes to eat dinner at Big Jim's whenever Shauna is working. When I had a break in my shift, I sat with Kelly. She quizzed me on the table numbers. It helped a lot.

Kelly also told me that Sadie almost fired Shauna once for not coming into work after she got into a car accident. "I still don't know why Shauna didn't just quit," Kelly said.

"I suppose she needs a job," I said.

"When you're right, you're right, Josie," she said with a smile. I had never heard anyone say that before, but I liked it. I like being right.

On top of learning the table numbers, I learned how to do all the other tasks we are supposed to do when we have time. I refilled customers' water glasses when the servers were busy. I wiped off tables and chairs when the bussers were busy. I even swept under tables and picked up broken crayons that kids had left behind. I also wiped off sticky menu after sticky menu.

I also learned that it is best for me to do whatever Sadie tells me to do, even if I do not agree with her. That is really hard for me.

Once, when my sister Janna picked me up from work, I complained to her about Sadie. She said, "Well, Josie, she is your boss, after all. She is allowed to tell you what to do."

"I know, but she is such a *bossy* boss!" I said to Janna.

Janna started laughing. "Josie! Do you know anyone else who's been called bossy before?" she asked me. I didn't think this was very nice. I knew Janna was talking about me.

"But I never mean to be bossy," I said to my sister. "I just think people should do what is right. Not like Sadie. She's mean. I'm not like that!" I was getting upset.

"I know you're not mean, Josie. But, you think you always know what is right. That isn't possible. Trying to make your roommate or anyone else do what *you* think is right can seem bossy...and not very friendly," Janna said. We were quiet for a few seconds, and she asked me if I understood what she meant.

I nodded my head. I didn't feel like talking anymore. I was upset that people thought I was bossy. I had heard it before, of course. But now that I was working for the world's bossiest boss, I didn't want anyone to call me that anymore.

When my sister dropped me off at home, I decided I would ask my roommate Emma if she thought I was bossy.

Emma thought for a few seconds before she answered me. Then she said, "I don't know."

"C'mon, Emma, answer me. Yes or no," I said.

"Okay, yes. You can be bossy," Emma said quietly.

I got up quickly and went to the refrigerator where our apartment rules were displayed. I took them down and walked back into the living room where Emma was sitting.

"Do you still want to follow these apartment rules? Maybe we should write new ones since you think I'm so bossy," I said meanly.

"No, Josie! We made those rules together. Remember how my sister kept saying we both had to agree to each rule. Remember?" Emma said. She was getting upset. I knew Emma did not like to fight.

"Okay. Well, I'm sorry if I am bossy," I said sincerely. I felt tired, so I said goodnight to Emma and went to bed.

A couple days later, after all the customers at work were gone, I saw Derek and Sadie sitting across from each other in one of the booths. Shauna and Flo were whispering to each other, so I asked them what was going on.

"He's quittin' if he's got a brain," said Flo. She says things in a funny way like that. Once she said, "Sadie's got a burr in her saddle today." I laughed because it sounded funny, but I don't think Flo was joking.

"I hope not," said Shauna. "If Derek leaves, Sadie will be the only manager. I don't think I can deal with that." Shauna looked at me and at Flo. Her face looked tired. I didn't tell her that, though. My mom and dad told me it isn't nice to tell someone that they look tired, even if they do.

Shauna and I were still wiping down menus when we heard Derek say, "It's the *way* you say it, Sadie!"

"I know that!" Sadie shouted back.

Derek kept going. "I don't think you do. You are rude to everyone here. You are nice to customers, but you treat all of us like we're your servants," he said. Sadie looked shocked. Then they noticed that a bunch of us had stopped working and had started listening to their conversation.

They got up and started to walk outside when Sadie said, "If you would all be so kind as to get back to work please, I would appreciate it." I don't think Sadie meant what she said, though. She never talked like that. Usually she would say something like, "Back to work!" or, "You're not being paid to do nothing!"

When I got to work the next day, I found Flo and asked her if Derek had quit.

"No ma'am. He's here. But Big Jim is comin' to town for a visit. Sadie and Derek were talkin' about fixin' up the restaurant when they started fussin' at each other yesterday," Flo said. "I hope Jim sets her straight."

"Me too," I said to Flo. "Wait. What do you mean by 'set her straight'?"

"Jim needs to tell Miss Sadie that she ain't the queen around here. She needs to treat us with respect," Flo said.

"Then, yes, I hope he sets her straight!" I said. Flo winked at me and walked away.

Big Jim turned out to be a very big man indeed. He may be the tallest person I've ever met. Like Keith said, he didn't talk very much, but he seemed kind.

Best of all, Sadie was much nicer while he was at the restaurant.

"I wonder what Jim has said to Sadie," Keith said one day toward the end of Big Jim's visit. "She's *never* this nice! Now we'll just have to wait and see how long the 'new Sadie' sticks around."

After Big Jim went back to Tampa, Sadie stayed nice—for almost a week. Flo said something about teaching an old dog new tricks. Shauna told me it meant that Sadie has been acting this way for so long, that it might be too hard for her to change. I thought that was sad. I wondered if I was an old dog. I wondered if I could learn to be less bossy. How would I even start? I wondered if people can change.

I wonder what you think...

What Do You Think?

1.   Do you think Josie could become less bossy?

2.   What kinds of changes would she need to make to become less bossy?

3.   Have you ever worked for a boss you didn't like? What didn't you like about that person?

4.   At the beginning of the story, many things in Josie's life were changing. Have you ever gone through a big change, like getting a new job or breaking up with someone? How did that feel?

5.   Do you think it makes sense for roommates to have rules to follow?

Story 3

The Mystery of the Missing Towels

GUESS WHO JUST SOLVED A MYSTERY? I did! I'm Emma the detective. My boss and my sister helped me, but I was the one who saw the most important clue. I've always liked to solve puzzles and find clues. I think it's because I read the *Nancy Drew Mystery Stories* when I was younger.

Nancy Drew is a detective. She lives with her father and housekeeper, and she solves all kinds of mysteries. Most people don't think a young woman like her can solve mysteries, but she does! Mysteries are still my favorite kind of stories to read.

There are a few things you should know before I tell you *The Mystery of the Missing Towels*. I work part-time at Riley's Rec Center near my apartment. "Rec" is short for *recreation*, which is how people spend their free time. Usually, people like to do fun things for recreation. People also exercise for recreation. Personally, I do not think exercising is fun. But like my younger sister Maggie always says, "Different strokes for different folks." This means it is okay for people to be different and like different things.

Speaking of Maggie, she is the best sister in the world. When I was growing up, it was hard for me to learn. I still get nervous when I have to learn something new. Maggie helped me a lot when I was in school. Now that we are grown up, she helps me with things like managing my money and getting around town.

Maggie is also one of my book club's helpers.

Guess who the other helper is? It's my brother Eddie! Eddie and Maggie are twins, and they're three years younger than I am. Maggie is a high school Spanish teacher. Eddie and his wife Nina just retired from the Marines and moved back to our hometown a month ago. Maggie and I were so excited when he told us he was moving back home! Nina was a nurse in the military, and she just got a nursing job at the hospital across town. Eddie plans to become a "security contractor" now. I think that means he will keep big office buildings safe, or something like that. I just love that I get to see my sister and brother at book club every week.

I have a roommate named Josie. Josie and I are different, but we get along. My sister helped us write rules for our apartment when I moved in with Josie. I follow the rules most of the time, and Josie reminds me when I forget.

I think being in a book club with Josie has helped us find more things in common. We both like to get to the end of a chapter before we stop reading for the day. Also, we like to order the same chai latte at Java House, the coffee shop where our club meets. Josie had never tried a chai latte before she smelled mine at book club. Now it's her favorite, too.

But, like I said, Josie and I are different. I do not like to tell people what to do. Josie can be bossy. Although, she is trying to change that. Another difference between Josie and me is that I haven't had a boyfriend yet. Josie has. Actually, one of Josie's ex-boyfriends is in our book club! Josie wasn't sure if she and Steve (that's his name) should be in the same club. She was worried that Steve would be rude to her. Maggie helped Josie and Steve decide on rules for how they would treat each other at book club. So far, they are getting along. I'm glad about that.

Now, back to the mystery! At my job at the rec center, I do a few different tasks. I say hello to members when they come into the gym. I go get things they ask for, like basketballs and volleyballs, from the storage closet. Then I ask them to write down what they borrowed on a clipboard that is always on the big desk where I sit. I keep the space around the big desk clean. I spend most of my time putting towels in and out of the washer and dryer. And then I fold the towels. I bet I have folded a million towels by now. Okay, maybe not a million, but I've folded *a lot* of towels! I fold them very neatly. Everyone says so.

Recently I went into the women's locker room to get the basket of dirty towels. I noticed that the stacks of clean towels I put on the locker room shelves earlier that day were almost all gone. I was surprised since there weren't many members in the gym that day. I thought, *Oh, well. The towels must be here somewhere.*

A couple days later, the same thing happened. There were only a few towels on the shelf in the women's locker room, but there weren't any in the dirty towel basket. *Well, this is strange*, I thought.

I decided that I should tell my manager, Robert. Later, when he walked past the big desk, I was folding towels as usual.

"Robert, I think I should tell you something," I said. All of a sudden I felt nervous. I hadn't done anything wrong. This wasn't good news, though. This could be bad news. I don't like to tell people bad news.

"Sure, Emma," Robert said. "What's up?"

"I think something is happening to our towels," I said.

"Something is happening to our towels?" Robert asked.

I nodded my head and kept talking. "A couple days ago, I noticed there were way fewer clean towels in the women's locker room than there should have been. It was a really slow day at the gym. Then it happened again today. Most of the clean towels are gone, but there aren't *any* towels in the dirty towel basket." I looked at Robert. I wondered if he believed me.

"Hmmm, that is strange," Robert said, scratching the big beard on his face.

"Maybe people are just using more towels?"

"I don't think so. There aren't more dirty towels in the basket than usual," I said. I wanted Robert to believe me, but I realized I didn't have any proof. Nancy Drew would always find proof that something wrong was happening.

"Okay. I believe you," Robert said. That made me feel better. Then he asked, "You don't count the towels before you put them in the women's locker room, do you?"

"No, I don't. Am I supposed to count them?" I asked.

"No, I've never counted the towels when I put them in the men's locker room. But how about we keep track over the next week? We'll put a piece of paper on the big desk. You track the towels for the women's locker room, and I'll track the towels for the men's locker room. Let's make a chart." Robert grabbed a notepad and made a chart.

On the chart were two columns. One was for the number of folded towels Robert put away in the men's locker room. The other column was for the number of folded towels I put in the women's locker room. Robert also suggested that we write the date and time next to the number of towels.

"Do you have any questions?" Robert asked. I shook my head. The chart was easy for me to understand. I was glad about that.

"All right then, Emma. Let's solve this mystery," Robert said.

"I like to solve mysteries!" I told Robert. Now I felt excited instead of nervous. I imagined I was Nancy Drew. I would solve the mystery of the missing towels. Work just got a whole lot more interesting.

After one week of tracking, Robert and I only knew *one* thing for sure. The towels were going missing from the women's locker room, not the men's.

It was going to be tough to figure out who was taking the towels. We couldn't search inside the women's gym bags. So I started paying closer attention to the women who came in and out of the gym.

Many women came in and out of the gym each day, and almost all of them carried a gym bag. I imagined the thief's gym bag bursting open on her way out of the gym because she filled it with too many towels. Then I would catch the thief "red-handed," like detectives say. That didn't happen though. I kept watching.

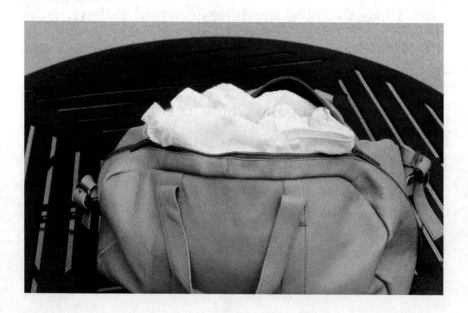

The Mystery of the Missing Towels

One of our gym members is Connie Connors. She comes in every day to use the steam room, and then she swims thirty laps in the pool. If you're swimming, you definitely need to use a towel. Maybe Connie was our culprit (the culprit is the person doing the bad thing). I couldn't imagine Connie stealing anything, though. She is so nice. She even sent the gym staff a fruit basket once!

Then there is Sandy Sanderson. She comes into the gym almost every day. But I don't know how much she uses the gym to work out. When I go into the locker room, I usually see her sitting on a bench looking at her phone.

Amy Apple is another member of the rec center. Amy is a successful business person in our town. She wears fancy clothes and carries a big fancy gym bag.

Laura Laredo is here all the time. I think she is a body builder. She carries a huge gym bag. Could Laura be stealing our towels?

Also, Robert and I couldn't figure out why anyone would need *so many* towels. At least twenty-five towels were missing! Robert guessed that maybe one of the women was working at a hotel that needed more towels. But then we remembered that our towels have the rec center logo on them. White towels with a bright blue Riley's Rec Center logo in the corner wouldn't look very nice in a hotel.

I couldn't think of *any* reason to take so many towels. I wondered if we would ever solve the mystery.

Then, two days ago, my sister Maggie picked me up from work. I like the days when I don't have to walk home. Maggie and I will usually do something together before she takes me home. Sometimes we go shopping. Sometimes we get something to eat. On this day, we were running errands. After we dropped off some mail at the post office, Maggie said she needed a car wash.

"Maybe I'll try the new car wash on Third Street," Maggie said. I didn't know about the new car wash, but I was happy to be along for the ride.

Maggie pulled into Amy's Wash and Wax. There were a few cars ahead of us in line, so we waited our turn. I watched as the newly washed cars came outside and two workers ran up to hand-dry them. They wiped off the windows and tires and everything. Then it was our turn.

"Here we go," Maggie said.

"Here we go," I said, too. We smiled at each other. When we were little kids, we loved to go through the car wash with our parents. The soap and water and giant round brushes were so noisy and messy. But we stayed nice and dry inside the car.

When we pulled out of the car wash, it was time for the car to be dried. The workers ran up to Maggie's car and reached to dry the top of the car. They were wiping off the windshield when I saw *it*.

"That's our towel!" I yelled so loudly that I scared Maggie.

"What are you talking about, Emma?" Maggie asked.

"Look at the towel! It's got the rec center logo on it! See?" I pointed to a towel that was being used to dry off the window right next to Maggie's face.

"No, I don't see anything but a white towel," Maggie said. "Why do you think this is the rec center's towel?"

"The blue logo! It's right there on the corner of the towel!" I pointed again.

"Oh my goodness. You're right. There it is!" Maggie said. "How did you spot it?"

"I have folded so many of those towels. I could spot that logo anywhere!" I said, feeling excited, then confused. "So the car wash took our towels? Why?"

"I'm not sure *who* took the towels. But it's easy to see *why* they were taken. A car wash would need a lot of towels," Maggie said.

"This is a break in the case!" I said, feeling like Nancy Drew. Except I wasn't sure what to do next. Should I call the police? Should I get out of Maggie's car and grab the stolen towels right out of the workers' hands? In the end, Maggie and I agreed that the best thing for me to do was call my boss, Robert. I didn't waste any time. I pulled my cell phone out of my purse and called the rec center.

"Riley's Rec Center," the person on the other end of the phone answered. I could tell it was Gayle. She always sounds like her nose is plugged up.

"Hi, Gayle. It's Emma. Is Robert there?" I asked.

"Oh hi, Emma. Didn't you just leave work?" Gayle asked.

"Yes, but I have news about the missing towels! Can I talk to Robert?" I asked. I was starting to feel impatient. I was so excited to tell Robert about my discovery.

"Hold on a second. I'll go get him," Gayle said.

While I waited for Robert to pick up the phone, the workers finished drying Maggie's car. Each of them held one of the rec center's towels as they smiled and waved at us.

"I'm going to have to drive away now," Maggie said. "But before I do, do you want to make sure those are *the* towels?"

"I know they are the towels. I'm positive," I said.

"Positive about what?" Robert said on the phone.

"Robert, I found the towels! Well, at least a few of them. But I bet they're all here!" I could hardly wait to tell him the story. I put him on speakerphone so Maggie could talk, too.

"Did you recognize any of the workers at the car wash?" Robert asked. I told him that I didn't.

"Which car wash is it again?" he asked.

This time Maggie answered. "It's the new one over on Third Street. Amy's Car Wash...or Amy's Wash and Wax. That's it. Amy's Wash and Wax. Do either of you know any Amys?" Maggie asked.

"Amy Apple!" Robert and I said at the same time.

"Whoa! Isn't she a wealthy business owner? Do you think she could be the towel thief?" Maggie asked.

"I'm already looking it up on the computer," Robert said. We could hear him typing as he searched for the owner of the new car wash on Third Street.

"Bingo," Robert said. "Amy Apple. I can't believe it."

"Me neither," I said. "What next?"

"We will need to file a police report," Robert said.

"Gosh, really? Could you just ask her to replace the towels instead?" Maggie asked.

"Or maybe we tell her she can't come back to the gym," I suggested.

"I would, but I'm looking at our employee manual right now. It says we have to report any theft to the police," Robert said, "even if it does seem a little harsh."

"Well then, that's what you have to do," Maggie said.

"Emma, would you be able to meet me at the police station in about ten minutes? I think they'll want to talk to the star detective," Robert said.

I looked at Maggie. She nodded her head. I told Robert I would meet him at the police station.

"This is too cool! You solved the mystery, Emma!" Maggie said.

I couldn't stop smiling. I *did* do it!

As we drove across town to the police station, Maggie and I wondered what the police would do next. We wondered if I would be on the news. We wondered why someone who was so successful would steal towels from the gym.

"Who knows," Maggie said. "I guess we never know how successful someone really is. Fancy clothes and cars don't tell the whole story."

"You mean someone like Amy Apple might not have enough money to buy towels for her new business?" I asked. This didn't make sense to me.

"Maybe. Her businesses may not be as successful as everyone thinks," Maggie said. "Or sometimes people steal because they have a mental health problem, and they can't stop themselves from taking things."

We pulled into the police station. Before we got out of the car, Maggie put her hand on my shoulder and said, "We don't know for sure that Amy Apple is the thief. I suppose the police will have to investigate. But no matter how this turns out, I hope you are as proud of yourself as I am of you, sister."

I smiled and nodded. I was proud. As we walked into the police station, I saw Robert sitting in the waiting area.

When he saw me, he raised his hand for a high five and said, "There she is. Our very own Nancy Drew!"

What Do You Think?

1.   Has anything of yours ever been stolen? If you want to share, what was it? How did it make you feel?

2.   In the story, Amy wore fancy clothes and carried a fancy gym bag. Is it easy or hard to know things about a person by the way they look?

3.   Do you have siblings? Do they live nearby? How often do you see each other?

Story 4

Tia's Tunes

I LOOKED AT THE CLOCK ON THE WALL. I didn't want to be rushed before my first gig. "Gig" is another word for a job, and my first gig as a DJ was coming up fast. I didn't think I would feel so nervous! My roommate Heather left early for work because she said my pacing was making her nervous, too. Do you ever do that when you're nervous? Just walk around? Well, I do. Finally, with only two hours to go, I decided it wasn't too early to start getting dressed.

A year ago, I decided I would try to make one of my dreams in life come true. I saved all the money I could to buy equipment to start my own DJ business.

I called it "Tia's Tunes" because my name is Tia, and tunes is another word for music. The main reason I decided to be a DJ is because I love music. I mean, I *really* love music.

When I moved into my own apartment, the very first thing I did was crank up my speaker so I could listen to my newest playlist on my phone. I'm lucky that my roommate likes music too. She doesn't like all the different kinds of music I do, so when she is home, I usually play the music she likes: pop music and a few "oldies" from Frank Sinatra and Elvis.

Personally, I appreciate almost every kind of music. I grew up listening to a lot of salsa and other Latin music with my parents. I still enjoy that music, but I really like Latin and American pop, hip hop, rap, and rock. I don't listen to jazz or classical music very often, but I understand why other people like that music. When I'm feeling good, I want to listen to music. When I'm feeling bad, I want to listen to music.

Music can pump me up, and music can relax me. When I'm with friends or family, I love playing a song that everyone likes. It's the best feeling! Everyone dances and sings along. Now that I am a DJ, I can make that happen for so many more people!

Another reason I started Tia's Tunes is because I wanted to make some extra money. I didn't charge any money the first two times I DJ'ed, since I was still learning how to use all the equipment. But now I was getting ready for my first paid gig, and the best part was that it was my cousin Lula's thirteenth birthday party.

In Spanish, *Tia* can mean "aunt" or "princess." But the real "princess" in my family is Lula. My aunt and uncle love to treat Lula to all the newest and nicest things. This year, Lula wanted to have a dance party for her birthday. When my aunt and uncle hired me to DJ the party, I was so excited!

I was still excited as I looked at my outfit for the party: jeans, my favorite slip-on, zebra-striped sneakers, and an aqua blue T-shirt that said "Happy 13th Birthday Lula!" Of course, aqua blue is Lula's favorite color. With the party only a couple hours away, I was also starting to feel nervous. A friend told me that sometimes *excited* can feel like *nervous*. I think that was how I was feeling.

I put on my headphones and played some peaceful music to help me relax while getting dressed for the party. Thankfully, my dad and I had set up all my DJ equipment at the front of Lula's dance floor the day before, so I didn't need to worry about that.

Another thing to know about me is that I have cerebral palsy, or CP for short. I was born with it. I don't know what life would be like without it. People with CP have trouble moving their muscles the way they want to. I have a very stubborn left hand that won't move the way I want it to. When I walk, it looks like I might lose my balance. I usually don't, though.

Also, my speech sounds a little slurred. When I was growing up, my parents and therapists taught me how to do things like pouring myself a glass of juice with only my right hand. They taught me to speak slowly and clearly.

My parents told me that CP can't stop me from going after my dreams, and I believed them. But there are still times when I wish I didn't have CP. Doing things like putting my hair in a ponytail can take a long time. My mom thinks I should get a short haircut to make things easier, but I like my long hair.

It takes me a lot longer to do everyday things like getting dressed and folding laundry. I get frustrated. "Why me?" I wonder. "Why do *I* have to have CP?" I don't stay upset for long, but it happens. My dad says it's okay to feel frustrated. Sometimes I feel downright sorry for myself, and I think that's okay, too.

I started getting ready for the party early because, like I said, it takes me longer to do things. I was also using a new app on my phone to help me get to and from places since I don't drive. It's called a rideshare service. I enter the address of the place I want to go, and a driver from the service picks me up and takes me. Then the money comes out of my bank account.

My parents worry about me using this. They worry about me a lot. I tell them that I like doing things independently when I can. I don't think they like it, but they respect my choices.

My aunt and uncle only live ten minutes away. Since I didn't want to feel rushed, I asked the driver to come a half hour before I needed to be there.

I looked at my watch. I only had twenty minutes to get dressed before the driver arrived. I'd already showered and done my hair and makeup, so the hard part was finished. Or *so I thought*. Now, all I needed to do was put on my clothes.

First, the T-shirt. I used my right hand to pull the shirt over my head and put my arms through the sleeves. Then, of course, I needed to comb my hair again. After that, I put on my jeans—one leg at a time, like my dad likes to say for some reason. I walked over and slid my feet into my comfy slip-on sneakers. They have zebra stripes *and* sequins. I love these shoes. Actually, I like most shoes. I would have a closetful if I could afford them!

Now all I needed to do was tuck in my T-shirt and zip up my jeans.

I don't know exactly how it happened. I tucked in my shirt, pulled the zipper of my jeans with my right hand, and worked hard to button the button, like always. Then I walked over to the mirror to look at myself. Sticking out of my zipper was the aqua blue T-shirt. It was a small piece of the fabric, about the size of a golf ball, but definitely noticeable. I rolled my eyes, sighed, and walked back over to my bed to undo and then redo the tucking, zipping and buttoning.

I pulled the zipper down until it stopped moving. It was stuck on the T-shirt, and it wasn't moving. I tried with all my strength to pull the T-shirt out, but it wouldn't move either. I closed my eyes and took a breath. I was stuck in a T-shirt and jeans that were stuck inside each other. What was I going to do? I thought, *If I could use both my arms and hands the way I need to, I wouldn't be in this situation. I hate CP. I hate it.* Then I just lay there and let myself cry for a couple minutes. I was *so frustrated.*

Then my phone beeped. I pulled it out of my back pocket and saw that the driver would arrive in two minutes. I went to the bathroom for a tissue to blow my nose. I wiped the mascara that had run down the sides of my face. But my T-shirt was still stuck in the zipper of my jeans, and now I couldn't even pull the zipper back up. My underwear were showing and I had no way to fix this on my own. I had to try hard not to cry and let my makeup run all over again.

All I could think to do was put on my big rain coat that would cover me up…and pray that someone at the party could help me with my zipper.

The driver was nice. She didn't say much, which was fine with me. I did not feel like chatting. I kept thinking to myself, *What a terrible start to the night, Tia! Mom and Dad are going to think I'm not ready for my own business if I can't even show up fully dressed to my first real gig.* I admit, I was not thinking positively. I was feeling sorry for myself and I didn't care.

I thanked the driver and got out of the car in front of my aunt and uncle's house. There was a huge "Happy Birthday" sign in the yard and balloons everywhere.

When I walked into the house, I tried to smile. My Aunt Patricia saw me first.

"Why are you wearing a rain coat on such a beautiful day, Tia? Aren't we lucky to have such lovely weather?" she asked. Aunt Patricia was cheerful, but I couldn't help it. Tears were coming down my cheeks as I walked over to her.

"Oh, Tia! What's wrong, sweetheart?" she asked me.

"Can we talk in private?" I asked.

"Of course," Aunt Patricia said, and we walked into her office on the first floor of the house. "Are you nervous? You're going to be great, Tia! I know it," my aunt said. Somehow, her kind words made me cry even more. So I just unsnapped my rain coat and showed her the whole situation, purple underwear and all. She looked concerned at first. But once she understood what was making me so upset, she gave me a big hug and told me not to worry. "We can fix this, Tia," she said. She rubbed my back and let me finish crying. I felt so thankful for her. Then Lula knocked on the door of the office.

"Mom! Is Tia here? Can I come in?" Lula asked excitedly. I could tell she was ready to get her party started.

"Tia is here, sweetheart. We just need to take care of something. We'll be out soon," Aunt Patricia answered. Then she looked up at me. "I'm going to try to pull the T-shirt out of the zipper, okay?"

I nodded my head. As Aunt Patricia pulled and tugged and tried everything she could to get the T-shirt out of the zipper, she said things like, "Hmmm," and "Gosh, this really is stuck," and, "I wonder if..." Finally, she walked over to her desk and grabbed a pair of scissors. "I think if I cut the T-shirt very close to where it is stuck, I can get the small bit of fabric out of the zipper. Is that okay with you?" she asked.

"Okay," I said. I was willing to try anything. Then I realized something. "But my new T-shirt will be cut! You and Uncle Julio just gave it to me," I said.

Patricia smiled and said, "Girl, don't worry about that." Just as quickly as my T-shirt got stuck in my zipper, Patricia made one cut and it was freed. "Okay, now for the next part," she said. She made lots of small cuts in the piece of fabric still stuck in the zipper. Little by little, my aunt cut that fabric into such a small piece that she was able to pull it out with her fingernails. She stood back, looked at me, and said, "Hurrah!"

I looked down and couldn't believe it. She did it!

"Thank you, Aunt Patricia! I can't believe you fixed it," I said. There was more knocking on the door.

"Come out of the office, please! I want to show Tia the backyard!" Lula was running out of patience.

"One more minute, Lula," Aunt Patricia said. Then she looked at me and asked, "Would you like me to help with the rest?" This was a kind offer. After all, my shirt was still untucked and my jeans were still unzipped. However, my aunt and uncle know how important it is to me that I do things independently.

I thought for a couple seconds. I knew I could do this on my own. I had gotten myself dressed more times than I could count. But I was still a little upset, so I said, "I think I can do it. But would you stay? Just in case?" Aunt Patricia nodded. I carefully tucked in my shirt and zipped up my jeans. "Phew!" I said. I felt so relieved. "I wouldn't mind help with the button," I said.

"You got it," Aunt Patricia said, with a smile on her face. She buttoned the button. We hugged again, and I told her how grateful I was for her and Uncle Julio.

"We're thankful for *you*, Tia," she replied. "Just one more thing," Aunt Patricia said as she licked her thumb and wiped the last bit of mascara that had run down my cheek from crying. I stopped letting my mom do gross things like that a long time ago. But at that moment, it felt kind.

"Okay, then. We've got a birthday girl and a whole lot of her friends ready to dance, and *you* are the DJ! Shall we?" Patricia waved her hand toward the door of the office.

"Yes," I said. "I'm ready. But first, would you mind not telling my mom and dad about this? They worry about me living on my own. I don't want them to think I can't do it." More knocking on the office door.

Patricia sighed. "Lula, we will be out when we are ready! Please go outside!" she shouted to Lula.

Then she looked at me with a serious expression on her face. "Tia, you are an adult who can make her own decisions. If you don't want me to tell your mom and dad, I won't. But I hope you know that they do believe in you. They worry because they are your parents. That is what parents do," she said.

"I know. Thank you, Aunt Patricia," I said. We heard a couple car doors shut. Patricia looked out the window and then looked at me.

"Boys and girls in aqua blue T-shirts are here. Time to get this party started!" she said.

I was ready. We walked to the backyard and I let the feelings of excitement come back. I wasn't nervous anymore. I was excited as I saw all of Lula's friends in their aqua blue T-shirts. I was excited as my uncle lit the tiki torches and turned on all the lights that were strung across the backyard. I was excited as I walked over to my DJ booth and turned on the equipment. Lula ran over and gave me a hug.

"What were you and my mom doing in her office for so long?" she asked.

"She was helping me with something," I answered simply. "Are you ready to dance?" I asked her. Before she could answer, I pushed a button, and the first song of the night started. It was Lula's favorite dance song. She squealed and ran to the dance floor to meet her friends. They danced and sang along. We were all happy.

What Do You Think?

1.   Have you ever thought about starting your own business? In this story, Tia's love for music made her want to be a DJ. Do you have any interests or hobbies that you would want to do as a job?

2.   We all need help in life. But sometimes we just want to do things on our own, like Tia does. Is there anything you need help doing that you want to do on your own?

3.   When is your birthday? Do you have a favorite birthday memory?

4.   What do you want to do on your next birthday?

Story 5

I Voted Today

Melvin is my name.
Being funny is my game.
I like to talk and laugh and make jokes.
Knock, knock...it's Melvin, folks!

HI! MY NAME IS MELVIN. Some people like to call me Mel. I don't mind, but I prefer Melvin. It was my grandpa's name. My dad says he was very funny.

My mom and dad couldn't have kids, so they adopted me. My birth mom had a hard life and couldn't raise a baby. So my mom and dad took me home. I'm so glad they did. I have a great life.

Well, I do have trouble with some things, like learning and paying attention. I don't hear very well, so I wear hearing aids. Also, it took me a long time to learn to talk. My mom says, "Once you learned to talk, you never stopped!"

I have these problems because I have something called Fetal Alcohol Spectrum Disorder. I guess my birth mom drank a lot of alcohol when she was pregnant with me. Sometimes I feel angry at her. But I don't even know her. My parents don't know her either. All they know is that she was very sad to give me up for adoption. I wish I could send her one of my funny poems. I bet she would laugh!

Now I have a story to tell you. Do you want to hear it?

Well, you can't! You have to read it!

It started a couple months ago at a *People in Action* meeting. You can be in *People in Action* if you have a disability like me and you want to learn to speak up for yourself. It's a cool group.

My favorite friend at *People in Action* is Tia. "Tia, Tia, who wouldn't want to be ya?" I say to Tia when I see her. She always smiles. Sometimes she laughs.

Tia is also in my Next Chapter Book Club, so I get to see her every Wednesday night. My book club is a cool group, too. I need help with reading. Other people need help with things, too. The cool thing is that we all help each other.

Like I was saying, I was at a *People in Action* meeting a couple months ago. A lady named Lenore visited to talk to us about voting. She works at something called the Board of Elections.

"Has anyone here voted in an election?" Lenore asked. I looked around. Some people raised their hands. Tia raised her hand.

I didn't raise my hand. I had never voted.

"Why is it important to vote?" Lenore asked.

A guy in the front row said, "Every vote counts!"

"That's right," Lenore said. "What's another reason to vote?" A woman near the window raised her hand.

"Voting is the best way to speak up for yourself," she said.

Lenore nodded her head. "You're right. Voting is how we tell our government what we want," Lenore explained. "We should also remember that not every adult in this country has always been allowed to vote. Some groups of people had to fight for their right to vote."

"Like women!" Tia said.

"Right, like women. Women have only been allowed to vote in U.S. elections for 100 years," Lenore said.

I didn't know that. I wondered why women wouldn't be allowed to vote. To tell you the truth, I never thought about voting that much. It didn't seem very interesting to me. Also, it's hard for me to learn new things. So I thought, *Why bother?*

"Now, let's talk about our rights and responsibilities when it comes to voting," Lenore said. "You have the right to have your vote counted correctly. You have the right to ask for and get help when voting. You have the right to decide who or what to vote for, without any pressure from other people."

I thought all of that sounded good. Maybe it was time to change my mind about voting.

Lenore went on.

"Voters also have responsibilities. It is your responsibility to learn about the candidates (the people who are running for election) and issues (like whether or not to give more money to schools) so you can make informed voting choices. You have the responsibility to know where your polling location is. A polling location is where you vote. It is usually near where you live. You also have the responsibility to bring personal identification, like a state-issued ID, with you to vote."

At the end of Lenore's talk, she showed us pictures of what it looks like to vote. We saw the website where you can register to vote. We saw pictures of people waiting in line, showing their ID cards, and standing in a voting booth. We saw a picture of a voting machine. It looked confusing. I didn't even know you used a *machine* to vote. I worried that voting might be too hard for me.

Before the meeting ended, a guy named Gary asked if he could read a poem he wrote. Lenore said it was our decision. We all agreed to listen to Gary's poem. He walked to the front of the room and said, "Hi everybody. I'm Gary, and my poem is called 'Give a Hoot.' I hope you like it."

Then he cleared his throat and began,
"Give a Hoot
Stand up for yourself or sit down
Give a hoot or turn around

Something's Brewing

Speak your mind all the time
Or take a place at the end of the line

Do you like being told what to do?
Or where to go or who to talk to?
Maybe it's time to speak your mind
Or wonder if you've been left behind

It's your choice
Use your voice
Or step aside
And let others decide

What do you want to be?
What do you want to do?
Do you want to be a sheep,
following the other guy?
Or do you want to be a leader,
reaching for the sky?

It may mean taking a risk
And maybe even shaking a fist
But it's your right
To have a great LIFE

So, pretend you are an owl
Give a hoot and a howl
It is what matters to *you*
That is important for you to do
The end."

Everyone clapped, and a couple people cheered. Lenore said, "Thank you, Gary! What a perfect way to end our talk about voting. Because when we give a hoot, we vote!"

When the meeting ended, I turned to Tia. "Cool poem, huh?" I said.

"Yeah, really cool!" Tia said.

"Tia, when did you start voting?" I asked.

"I learned about voting in social studies. When I turned eighteen, I registered on the website and got my voter registration card in the mail. That's what tells you where you're supposed to vote. I vote at a church near my house. It's easy. The worst part is waiting in line," Tia said.

"I want to vote," I said. "But I'm afraid I won't know how to use those machines. What if I mess up?"

"There are people who can help you with the machines. Plus, you can start over if you need to," Tia said. "It happened to me once. It wasn't a big deal. I think you should vote, Melvin."

"I want to, but I'm going to need some help," I said.

Tia pointed to the table at the front of the room. "Go get one of those handouts. It has all the steps listed on it," Tia said.

"Thanks, Tia," I said.

"You're welcome," Tia said. "My ride is here. I have to go. See you at book club on Wednesday!"

"See ya, Tia!" I said.

I walked up to the table and took one of the handouts. When I went outside, my staff Gil was waiting in his car for me. As soon as I got inside the car, I handed Gil the piece of paper.

"What is this?" Gil asked.

"I want to learn to vote. I want to be a voter," I said. Saying that made me feel good. I knew I was making the right choice.

Gil nodded his head as he read the words on the paper. He smiled and said, "Right on, man. Do you want me to help?"

"Yes, please," I said.

"You got it. Voting is a big deal. I'm excited for you, Mel," Gil said. I smiled all the way home.

When I got inside, the first thing I said to my mom and dad was, "I'm going to learn to vote and Gil is going to help me."

"That's excellent," my mom said. "Is this what you talked about at the *People in Action* meeting?"

I nodded my head.

"Great choice, Melvin," my dad said. He walked over and gave me a hug. My dad gives the best hugs.

Melvin is learning something new.
Learning is hard for him to do.
It makes him want to spew.
But he will give it his best shot.
After all, why not?
It's better to vote than to not.

The next day, Gil and I went to the library to use the computer. We found the website to register to vote. Gil helped me to type in all my information. I was on my way.

Over the next couple of weeks, I talked with my mom and dad and Gil about the people who were running in the election. I also learned about two issues I would vote on. One was something called a "levy" for our schools. This means the schools need more tax money. The other issue was about a new apartment complex. Some people wanted to build it near the town square. Other people did not want that to happen. I had decisions to make!

The coolest thing was when I got to practice on a voting machine. I don't know how Gil found it, but I'm happy he did. Using the machine wasn't as hard as I thought it would be. It was actually pretty easy! Practice can really help. I was starting to feel even more excited about voting.

A week before Election Day, my voter registration card came in the mail.

"Hey, Mom!" I yelled as I opened the envelope. "I got my card!"

"What card?" she asked.

"My voting card! Let's see, where do I vote? Tia and Gil said the card tells you where you vote," I said as I looked at the card. But I didn't see it right away. There were lots of words on the card and the letters were really small. I handed the card to my mom.

"Mill Creek Middle School," she said. "That's where your dad and I vote! We can all go together if you want," my mom said. She seemed excited. I wanted Gil to take me to vote, but I didn't want to hurt my mom's feelings. I decided I would be honest.

"Mom, if it's okay with you, I want Gil to take me to vote," I said.

"Of course it's okay, son. I'm proud of you for saying what you really want. It seems like you're learning a lot of new things," my mom said.

My mom is proud of me
It makes me want to sing with glee
You should hear me sing a song
Don't worry, it won't take long

I Voted Today

Get ready to be impressed
My voice is the best of the best!

My mom tells me that I shouldn't brag about myself. She says it isn't polite. *She* brags about me all the time! She tells people that I am kind and loving and funny. Plus, now I know how to vote! What will she say about me now?

Election Day was finally here. I was ready. I had a piece of paper in my wallet that I could use if I forgot which way I wanted to vote. Gil picked me up right on time, and we went to Mill Creek Middle School. Gil was already wearing a sticker that said "I Voted Today." I couldn't wait to get my sticker.

When we got to the school, it felt strange to be there again. Mill Creek Middle School is where I went to school. School wasn't the easiest time for me. I had lots of friends, but I did not get good grades. At least no one would be grading my votes!

That is another thing I learned about voting: my votes are private. I don't have to tell anyone how I vote.

When Gil and I got close to the cafeteria where the voting machines were set up, we saw a long line.

"I'm glad the line is inside, not out in the cold," Gil said.

"Oh man, that would be a bummer if we had to wait out in the cold!" I said.

The lady in front of me in line turned around and said, "A few years ago, I waited over two hours out in the cold. Then I spent another hour in line once I got inside!" A man in front of her shared about a time when he waited an hour in the rain to vote. All of a sudden, we had a nice group chat while we waited. It helped to pass the time. Soon, it was almost my turn to go into the cafeteria and vote.

I peeked inside and saw the voting machines. Uh-oh.

"Those are different machines, Gil," I said. "I don't know how to use those machines!"

"It'll be okay, Mel. You're right, they don't look like the machine we practiced on. But you will do the same things on this machine that you did on the other one. Don't forget, you can always ask for help," Gil said.

He put his hand on my shoulder. "I'll be right out here in the hall if you need me. You're ready. You got this," he said.

"Thanks," I said. I didn't feel ready. I worried I would push the wrong buttons and mess up everything. Why couldn't all the voting machines be the same? Maybe voting wasn't for me after all.

A woman at the check-in table called for the next person. I walked up to the table, took my ID out of my wallet, and handed it to the woman. She took it and looked up at me.

"Well hello, neighbor!" she said with a big smile. My face must have looked confused, because she asked, "You're Melvin, right?"

Now I really was confused. Of course I was Melvin. It said so right there on my ID.

"I'm Mary Jo. I live on the same street as you," she said.

"Oh," I said. "Hello, neighbor." I was so nervous I had already forgotten her name. She seemed like a nice lady.

"Well, you're here to vote, not to chat with me.

Let me get you checked in. Then I'll show you to your machine." She flipped through a stack of papers and found my name and address. "Sign here, please," she said as she pointed to a line with a big "X" in front of it.

After I signed my name, she stood up and asked me to follow her. The closer we got to the strange voting machines, the more nervous I got.

"What is your name again?" I asked.

"I'm Mary Jo. If you need help, all you have to do is ask," she said. I was glad she said that, especially since I was sure I'd need help.

Mary Jo put her hand on top of an empty voting machine. "Here you go, Melvin. Do you know how to use a voting machine?"

I was about to tell her how I had practiced on a different kind of voting machine. I was about to tell her that I would probably need a lot of help.

I walked around to the front of the machine. I couldn't believe it. This machine looked almost exactly like the one Gil and I had used! It was just a different shape and color on the *outside*. I felt like shouting for joy. "Phew!" I said, louder than I meant to.

"Is everything okay?" Mary Jo asked.

"I'm okay," I said. I felt confident now. "This is my first time voting, but I know how to do this."

"Wonderful! I'm so glad you're here," Mary Jo said.

"Thanks," I said. "Time to vote." I pointed to the machine. Mary Jo nodded and walked back to the check-in table.

Since votes are private, I won't tell you who I voted for. I will tell you that I voted "yes" on both of the issues. I think it would be good to give the schools more money. I also think it would be super cool to live in a new apartment near the town square.

When I was finished voting, I felt really proud. On my way out of the cafeteria, I waved goodbye to Mary Jo. "Nice to see you," I said.

"Nice to see you, too! Don't forget your sticker," she said, holding out one of the "I Voted Today" stickers.

"Thanks!" I said. I put the sticker on my shirt and walked out to meet Gil in the hallway.

As soon as Gil saw me, he raised his hand for a high five. "Way to go, man!" he said.

I felt so good, I raised both hands. "How about a high ten instead of a high five?"

Why high five when you can high ten?
Spread cheer to all the women and men
Why not vote when you have the right?
Take it from me, voting is out of sight!

What Do You Think?

1. Have you voted in an election? What was it like? Was it easy or hard to do?

2. Melvin learned to do something new, even though learning is hard for him. Have you ever challenged yourself to learn something new? If so, what was it?

3. Melvin and his friend Tia are part of a group called *People in Action*. Groups like this help people with disabilities learn to advocate for themselves. What does it mean to advocate for yourself? How important is it to advocate for yourself?

4. Melvin thinks he is pretty funny. Did you think he was funny? How about you? Are you funny? Do you have any jokes to tell?

Story 6
My Friends at Java House

GEEZ, IT WAS HOT TODAY. I could hardly think of anything other than the heat as I walked to my weekly Next Chapter Book Club meeting at the Java House. I also thought about the big iced coffee I would buy once I got to book club. I looked at my phone to find out exactly how hot it was; my weather app said 93 degrees. One of my friends in book club loves really hot weather. I tell her, she can have it! I wiped my face with a handkerchief and kept walking toward the main street I had to cross before I got to the Java House.

I know a lot about my friends from book club. We meet every week for an hour and take turns reading whatever book we've picked. We also talk about things going on in our lives. Tia, my friend who loves hot weather, just started her own business as a DJ. I think that's pretty cool. Before my accident, I was really into music. Classic rock, mostly. I still like music, but I don't listen as much as I used to.

Melvin is my best friend from Next Chapter Book Club. He makes me laugh! I don't always think his jokes are funny, but *he* does, and that always makes me laugh.

Steve is another friend from book club. Sometimes he gets frustrated by all the noise in Java House, so he takes a break and goes for a walk. That seems to help him. Walking helps me when I'm frustrated, too.

Steve's ex-girlfriend, Josie, is another member of our book club. Josie has a lot of ideas and opinions and likes to tell people what to do.

I think she is pretty smart, but I haven't told her that. She works full time at a restaurant and usually smells like barbecue when she comes to book club. I don't mind, though. I love barbecue!

Josie's roommate Emma is also in our book club. She loves to read mysteries and drink chai lattes. Emma is very nice. Secretly, I wonder if she might be *too* nice. Josie can be bossy sometimes!

Emma's brother and sister, Eddie and Maggie, are part of our club, too. Plus, they're twins! Eddie and Maggie are the facilitators for our book club. They meet us at Java House each week and help us when we need help.

My name is Owen, and I work full time at a big hardware store around the corner from my apartment. I stock shelves, help customers, and usually have a pretty good time at work. I've been working there for six years, and I have become friends with a few of my co-workers.

One friend from work actually calls me an hour before my shift starts to make sure I'm getting ready for work. I have trouble remembering things and organizing my time, so my friend helps me out by calling me. I really appreciate it. Also, Melvin calls me two hours before book club every Wednesday afternoon. I don't usually forget about book club, but since it is really easy for me to get distracted, Melvin gives me a call.

Sometimes I get confused and forget what day of the week it is. It is frustrating when things like this happen, but ever since my bike accident, it is just part of life. When I was nineteen, I was hit by a car while riding my bike. I broke my left leg and a couple ribs and hit my head on the pavement. I wasn't wearing a helmet. When I woke up, I was in an ambulance, and I didn't know how I got there. The doctor told me that I had been in an accident.

She said that after someone has a "traumatic brain injury" like mine, they can have a lot of problems with things like remembering, staying organized, and paying attention to people. The doctor also said it is common for people with brain injuries to get frustrated because it can be hard to communicate with other people. At least, this is what my sister *told* me the doctor said. I don't remember much about those first few days after the accident.

Unfortunately, the doctor was right; talking to people can be frustrating for me. If I am able to focus on what someone is saying, I may not understand it. If I do understand it, I may not be able to find the words I want to say back to the person. Since my injury isn't something other people can see from the outside, they may not understand why I'm frustrated. Over the years, I have gotten much better at asking people to slow down when they talk.

I also get headaches a lot. Sometimes I feel dizzy and off-balance. I don't ride a bike or drive a car anymore. Thankfully, I have an apartment that is near the places I need to go, so I walk almost everywhere.

I was a pretty popular guy before my accident. I had a lot of friends and liked to go out and party. Did I mention that I was drunk when the car hit me on my bike? Well, I was. I like to remind people that at least I wasn't *driving a car* drunk. The police said that I crossed a street on my bike when it wasn't my turn, and that is when the car hit me. When you're drunk, it is easy to make bad choices like I did that day on my bike. So I don't drink alcohol anymore. It makes my brain even more confused—not helpful!

Like I was saying, before the accident, I had a busy social life. For a while after the accident, I was very depressed. It took a long time for me to recover and be able to take care of myself. During that time, I didn't want to see or talk to people.

It only made me feel embarrassed and frustrated. Everything was so confusing and overwhelming.

But now, it has been almost thirty years since the accident. I have learned how to work around the challenges I have, like having my co-worker call me before my shifts at work. I still get confused and distracted easily. But I have lived with these problems for a long time now. I'm pretty good at knowing when I'm having trouble because of my injury, and I'm much kinder to myself when I do have trouble.

I used to be so hard on myself. That doesn't help any more than alcohol does. I've worked to make new friends and be social with people. When I'm with good friends, it makes me feel more like my old self.

I reached the stoplight and waited for it to change. I wiped my neck with my hankie. All I could think about was getting inside the air conditioning at Java House. It felt like I had been standing there for an hour, so I decided to think about the book our club is reading, *A Wrinkle in Time*. It's different than most of the books we've read. The characters are strange and funny, but the story gets confusing sometimes. Maggie said we can go to her house to watch the movie of *A Wrinkle in Time* after we finish the book. Maybe then I'll understand what this book is about!

Finally, the stoplight turned and I saw the sign that signaled it was okay for me to cross the street.

Screeeeeech!

All of a sudden, there was a white van stopped right in front of me. It was close enough for me to touch. I looked up and saw the driver. He looked stunned. I felt stunned too.

"Hey, man! Are you okay?" the driver yelled as he was getting out of the van. "I'm so sorry! I didn't see you in the crosswalk! I thought I could turn right; then all of a sudden, there you were! Oh man, I think my heart stopped…" He kept talking, but I had stopped listening. I walked quickly back to the sidewalk where I had been standing just a few moments ago.

The man followed me. He wanted to know if I was okay. "Yeah, I'm fine," I said. "Just a little shaken up."

"No doubt!" he said. "Are you sure you aren't hurt?" Cars began to honk and drive around the man's van that was stopped in the intersection.

"I'm sure," I said. "You can go." I didn't want his van to cause an accident, and I just wanted to get to book club and sit down.

The man got back in his van, and I waved at him so he would know I was okay. But, I *wasn't* okay. My body wasn't hurt, but I was starting to feel really weird.

I waited for the next green light and sign that it was my turn to cross the street. This time, I looked both ways before I stepped into the crosswalk. No cars were coming. I walked quickly across the street. My heart was pounding. Finally, I reached Java House, opened the door, and saw my book club sitting at their usual table.

"Hey, dude. Are you okay?" Melvin asked when he saw me.

I shook my head. The van didn't hit me, but I could tell that I wasn't okay. Maggie walked over to me and looked at my face.

"Owen, did something happen? Maybe you should sit down. Emma, would you go get Owen a glass of water?" She was nervous, I could tell. Tia started walking toward me. I didn't feel like talking, though. I just needed to sit down. In fact, I needed to sit down *right away*. I felt like I was going to faint. I sat down on the nearest chair and put my head between my knees.

By this time, everyone in the club had walked over and was standing around me. I hated the idea of causing a scene. I managed to say, "I'm okay. I just need space." Maggie quickly asked everyone to sit back down. Emma brought me a glass of water and went back to the table. Maggie stayed with me.

"Owen, I'm concerned. Would you like me to call 911?" Maggie asked.

"No!" I said, louder than I meant to. "I mean, no thank you. I'll be okay. Something just happened and I'm shaken up." I took a drink of cold water. It felt good. I was starting to feel less dizzy.

"What happened, Owen?" Maggie asked again.

"I was crossing the road and a van almost hit me," I said. "It didn't hit me, though. I don't know why I feel like this."

Maggie touched my shoulder, and I looked up at her. "Owen, do you think it might have something to do with your bike accident? Maybe this brought back some of those bad memories, and your body thinks you're still in danger," Maggie suggested.

"Maybe," I said. It made sense. I took another drink of water. "I'm okay," I said and started to stand up. Maggie stopped me.

"Why don't you sit here for a few more minutes," she said.

"We're not in a hurry. Right, guys?" Maggie called over to the group.

Everyone said "no" except for Steve, who said, "I'd like to get started."

"We need to give Owen a little more time," Emma told him.

"Fine, but we may not make it to the end of the chapter tonight if we don't start soon," Steve said, looking at his watch.

"Who cares?" Tia said. "Owen is our friend, and he is more important."

I was starting to feel normal again. I looked at Maggie. "I'm good. Really. Thank you for looking after me." I walked slowly to the table and sat in my usual seat. Maggie walked close behind me to make sure I didn't fall.

"What happened, man?" Melvin asked. "I couldn't hear what you and Maggie were talking about."

"It's okay, Mel. It has to do with my bike accident," I said.

"Wasn't that thirty years ago?" Steve asked. Steve seemed to remember everything.

"It was," I answered. "But just now a van almost hit me when I was crossing the street. It brought back a lot of scary feelings from the accident. I'm feeling better now, though."

"Great, let's start reading," Steve said, pointing to his watch.

"Hang on," Maggie said. "Owen, would you like to talk about how you're feeling? It might help," she suggested. But I didn't want to talk or think about my accident. I just wanted to read.

"No, let's start reading," I said. "I'd rather not think about my accident anymore."

"What accident?" Josie asked. I forgot that she was the newest member of our club. She didn't know my story.

I took a deep breath, and asked for what I needed. "If I promise to tell you about it some other time, can we start reading?" I asked.

"Sure, let's get started. I read first last week, so it's Melvin's turn to read first this week. We're on chapter ten, Melvin," Josie said. She was good at taking charge, and right then I was grateful for it.

Melvin began reading with help from Maggie. Tia showed Emma what page we were on. Josie's bookmark fell off the table, and Steve bent over and picked it up. I opened my book and settled in. It was good to be with my friends at book club.

What Do You Think?

1.   Have you ever had a serious accident or health problem? If so, how has it impacted your life?

2.   Do you belong to a club or group? If so, what are the different people in your group like? Do you consider the people in this group to be your friends?

3.   If you had a problem, who would you turn to for help?

A Note from Maggie and Eddie

HELLO, AND WELCOME to the second half of the book! The people you got to know in the first six stories (Steve, Josie, Emma, Tia, Melvin, and Owen) appear together in the following six plays. They are also joined by us, Maggie and Eddie. We're twins and younger siblings of book club member Emma. We also co-facilitate this awesome book club, and we look forward to meeting our friends at Java House every Wednesday night.

If you are reading these plays in a book club or with another group of friends, it can be a lot of fun to pick one or two of the characters in each play, read only their lines, and even act out how you think that character might sound. Give it a try!

We wish you happy reading!

Maggie and Eddie

Play 1

A Quick Buck

CHARACTERS

Eddie	Josie
Maggie	Steve
Tia	Melvin
Owen	Emma
Narrator	Older Woman

(The narrator tells the readers what the characters are doing. This person reads all *italicized*, or *slanted*, words.)

<u>Act I</u>

<u>Narrator</u>: *This is a play. Plays can be acted out on stage or read by members of a Next Chapter Book Club. We begin this play at a Wednesday night book club meeting. Eddie is the last person to arrive. He looks at his watch to make sure he isn't late.*

<u>Eddie</u>: Hey, everyone! I like this crew. You're all here on time!

<u>Josie</u>: Actually, Emma and Maggie and I were here ten minutes early.

<u>Maggie</u>: That's true, brother. You look a little stressed. How's the new house treating you and Nina?

<u>Narrator</u>: *Eddie shakes his head and rubs his neck.*

<u>Eddie</u>: There's nothing *new* about that house. But we like it. I can't believe how much stuff we have. We've been unpacking and decorating for weeks, and I'm tired! I'm not as young as I used to be.

<u>Steve</u>: Well, none of us is as young as we used to be.

<u>Josie</u>: Technically, Steve is right.

Eddie: I hear you. What I mean is that my body doesn't work as easily as it used to. I can't imagine getting through twelve weeks of boot camp now!

Tia: I can't imagine *ever* getting through twelve weeks of boot camp!

Narrator: *Everyone chuckles.*

Eddie: We have too much stuff! I keep trying to convince Nina to have a yard sale. She says we don't need one more thing to do right now. I get it, but I'd love to get rid of some of this stuff.

Melvin: My neighbors just had a yard sale. I bought some of their old CDs.

Owen: Cool, man. What did you get?

Melvin: Rock and roll. One CD is Pearl Jam. I forgot the others.

Owen: Nice. Pearl Jam is good stuff.

Tia: I like Pearl Jam too, but I don't play them much as a DJ. Everybody wants me to play dance music. I have a bunch of old CDs I've copied onto my computer that I could get rid of. Maybe I'll bring them to book club, and you can take what you want?

Owen: That's really nice, but wouldn't you rather sell them and make some money?

Steve: I'd buy any old Bon Jovi or Journey CDs you have.

Josie: I have an idea!

Narrator: *Everyone turns and looks at Josie.*

Josie: What if we all have a yard sale together?

Maggie: That's a great idea, Josie! Each of us can bring stuff we want to sell. We can have it at my house.

Eddie: If you're serious, I've got a truckload of stuff to bring. Maybe two!

Maggie: Great! What do the rest of you think?

Tia: I think it would be fun! I could sell my CDs.

Josie: I have lots of kitchen stuff to sell.

Maggie: Emma, do you have anything you'd want to sell?

Emma: Maybe some clothes. I'm running out of room in my closet.

Maggie: All right, cool. Steve, what about you?

Steve: I don't know. I'll ask my mom and dad.

Melvin: Me too, I'll ask my mom and dad.

Owen: Well, I'm in. I'm sure I have stuff in my apartment I don't need anymore, and I could definitely use a quick buck!

Melvin: What's a quick buck?

Owen: When you make money without having to work too hard for it, it's a quick buck.

Melvin: Cool! I want a quick buck!

Maggie: Well, we will have to do *some* work to make those bucks. But if we all help each other, it shouldn't be too bad. Let's start by picking a date. Usually, yard sales are on weekends. Since some of you work on weekends, we should pick a date at least a month from now to give you time to ask your bosses not to schedule you on that day.

Josie: Right. My manager Sadie makes us give at least three weeks' notice if we can't work a certain day. I think you all know how strict she is!

Emma: It's true. She's strict. You better ask her tomorrow, Josie!

Eddie: I suppose we should go ahead and look at our calendars? How about one month from this Saturday?

Narrator: *A few people pull out their phones to look at their calendars.*

Owen: I don't have a calendar on my phone.

Melvin: Me neither.

Tia: Here, Melvin, you can look on my phone.

Josie: Owen, do you want to look at my phone with me?

Narrator: *Eventually, everyone is looking at a calendar. The group agrees to have the yard sale one month from Saturday. Josie writes the date down for Melvin and Owen who don't have calendars on their phones.*

Tia: Everyone, make sure you tell your parents or whoever drives you places so they can put it on their calendars, too. What else do we need to do?

Eddie: Sounds like it's time for another to-do list.

Narrator: *For the next five minutes, the group talks about the things they need to do to prepare for a yard sale. Josie writes the to-do list and reads it to the group.*

Josie: Here goes:

- Sort through your home (closets, drawers, cabinets, etc.) for things you no longer want.
- Decide if those things are nice enough to sell. No trash!
- Decide on a price for each item and write it down. Maggie will have different colored stickers for each person to use as price tags.
- Bring your items to Maggie's the Friday night before the sale so you can make price stickers and put them on your items.

- Remember, yard sale prices are MUCH lower than what you paid in the store. Be open to pricing suggestions.
- Arrive at Maggie's by 7:00 a.m. on the day of the sale to pull everything out of the garage and be ready to greet customers at 8:00 a.m. Bring a folding chair if you have one.

Eddie: Sounds like a plan!

Josie: I'll bring copies of this list for everyone next Wednesday.

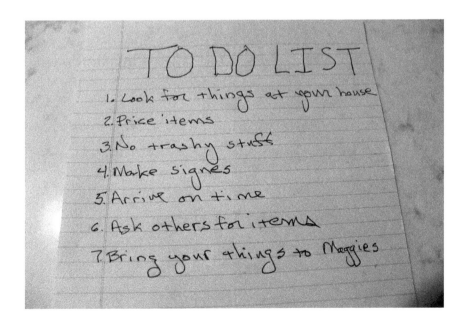

Owen: Good thinking, Josie.

Tia: I'm excited! I've never had a yard sale before.

Maggie: It's been a long time for me. I think I'll use any money I make to do something fun. Maybe something I've never done before.

Eddie: I see a new fishing pole in my future.

Emma: More stuff for your house?

Eddie: Good point, Em. I suppose I could save the money.

Steve: Are we going to read today? We only have a half hour left.

Maggie: Wow, have we been talking for a half hour already? Any other yard sale questions before we start reading?

Narrator: *Everyone is quiet, so Maggie motions to Steve, who is the first person to read that day. Steve takes his turn reading, but most people are distracted by what they want to do with their yard sale money.*

Act II

Narrator*: Throughout the next month, each book club member gathers the items they want to sell at the yard sale. The night before the sale, everyone brings their sale items to Maggie's house so they can put price tags on them. Melvin, Steve, and Josie each bring one big box of things to sell. Tia brings two boxes of CDs and some old posters. Owen brings an old suitcase full of things from all over his apartment. Emma brings two big bags of clothes and shoes to sell. Eddie brings a truckload of things, as he said, including five boxes, small pieces of furniture, and an old ping pong table. On his way home, he drives around and posts signs in the neighborhood to advertise the yard sale.*

The next morning, Tia is the last person to arrive at Maggie's. Her dad waves and wishes everyone good luck as he pulls away.

Tia is carrying her folding chair and a wide, flat box. Emma meets her at the end of the driveway and offers to carry the box.

Emma: What's in the box, Tia? Did you forget to bring something last night?

Tia: No, these are donuts.

Emma: Awesome! Thanks, Tia! Hey everyone, Tia brought donuts!

Eddie: Emma, you can bring that box right over here. I'm sure the rest of you don't want any, do you?

Steve: I do!

Josie: Me too!

Eddie: You mean I'm supposed to share?

Emma: Very funny, Eddie!

Narrator: *Emma puts the donuts on a table inside the garage. Everyone crowds around the donuts and reaches in to grab one.*

Maggie: It's like you all haven't eaten in a year! How about I go grab some napkins?

Tia: Good idea. Owen already has powdered sugar on his nose!

Owen: Oh, I meant to do that.

Narrator: *Owen adds more powdered sugar to his nose, and everyone laughs. Maggie returns with napkins and tells everyone to help themselves to water and coffee sitting on a shelf at the back of the garage.*

Melvin: Thank you for the donuts, Tia. I was hungry!

Steve: So was I. Thanks, Tia. I love blueberry donuts.

Tia: You're welcome, everyone. I hope we all make a lot of money today.

Josie: Hey look! There's a car pulling up already. Is it time to start?

Eddie: Well, it's not 8:00 a.m. yet, but serious bargain shoppers start early. Is everyone ready for business?

Narrator: *Everyone shouts, "Ready!" and startles the older couple walking up the driveway.*

Older Woman: My, you are an energetic group! That's good. Hopefully you can make a lot of sales before the rain starts today!

Steve: Rain? Did you say rain?

Older Woman: Oh yes, it's going to rain today.

Maggie: I suppose we watched different weather forecasts. Channel 3 said there was only a 20 percent chance of pop-up showers. Did you hear something different?

Older Woman: No, but my bones and joints tell me when it's going to rain. I'm sorry to tell you, but my hips are telling me there's a 100 percent chance of rain today.

Narrator: *The woman walks over to look at Emma's sweaters and coats. Steve and Maggie look up at the sky, searching for rain clouds, while everyone else looks at each other with worry.*

Older Woman: Such pretty sweaters! Will you take two dollars for this white one?

Emma: Um, how about three dollars? I will take three dollars for it.

Older Woman: It's a deal. This will look pretty on my granddaughter. Don't you think so, Frank?

Narrator: *The woman holds the sweater up for her husband to see. He nods his head. They walk around the yard and pick out a small lamp of Eddie's and a teapot from Owen's things. They pay Maggie for them in the garage. As they walk to their car, two more cars park in front of Maggie's house.*

Steve: I think that woman was wrong. I checked the weather on my phone last night, and there's only a slight chance of rain.

Eddie: Just in case, I'll go grab some tarps from the back of my truck.

Josie: Who ever heard of someone's hips predicting the weather?

Melvin: Not me!

Emma: Me neither.

Steve: *Now* my weather app says there are pop-up showers in the area. It didn't say that last night!

Tia: Should we move things into the garage?

Maggie: How about we keep an eye on the sky for now. If it seems like it's about to rain, we'll bring the tables inside the garage. Eddie's tarps can cover whatever we can't fit inside the garage. But for now we're in business!

Narrator: *Maggie points to the yard. More customers have arrived.*

Josie: Oh look, I think I might have a buyer for my jewelry box!

Owen: And that guy is looking at my old board games.

Narrator: *Over the next two hours, the yard sale is busy. The book club members forget about the chance of rain. They have fun meeting new people and making some money. Then, a low rumble of thunder catches everyone's attention. They gather on the driveway to look at the sky.*

Act III

Narrator: *Suddenly, there is a very loud clap of thunder.*

Josie: Okay, I think it might be time to move the rest of our things into the garage.

Tia: I agree!

Maggie: So do I. We have four tables to move. Let's each grab an end of a table and carefully walk them into the garage.

Eddie: Steve, can you help me move the ping pong table? It's pretty heavy.

Steve: Sure.

Narrator: *In just a few minutes, the book club members move the tables into the garage. It's a tight squeeze, but everything fits inside except a coffee table that Eddie brought. He covers it with a tarp just as the rain starts to pour down. Everyone huddles in the garage to watch the rain.*

Owen: I guess that lady's aching hips were right.

Maggie: I guess so! How about we take advantage of the break and go inside to rest for a few minutes?

Emma: Sounds good to me.

Melvin: Me too.

Narrator: *Everyone gathers around the dining room table to finish off the donuts. Maggie makes another pot of coffee.*

Josie: Wow, it's really raining hard!

Owen: Since we're stuck inside, maybe we could count the money each of us has made so far?

Tia: I've only sold a few CDs, so I don't think I've made very much.

Maggie: Didn't you see that someone bought your old microphone and speaker? You may have made more than you think, Tia. I'll go get the cash box and notebook from the garage.

Eddie: Who knows what they are going to do with the money they make today?

Melvin, **Steve**, and **Tia** *at the same time*: I do!

Tia: Melvin, what are you going to buy?

Melvin: I want to go see a comedy show. If I make enough money, I'm going to buy tickets to see the next big comic who comes to town.

Eddie: What a fun idea, Melvin.

Steve: I'm going to play the lottery with my money.

Josie: Really? Are you still playing the lottery?

Steve: I am, and you don't need to worry about it.

Narrator: *Josie puts her hands in the air to show Steve that she isn't going to ask him any more questions.*

Maggie returns with the cash box and notebook. She begins counting and making notes.

Tia: I want to buy a sign that says "Tia's Tunes" for the front of my DJ booth. Maybe something sparkly!

Emma: Cool, Tia. You all have such good ideas. All I thought of was going shopping at the mall.

Tia: That's a great idea. You *did* sell a lot of clothes today!

Emma: I guess you're right! What about you, Josie?

Josie: I want to go apple picking in the fall. My mom and dad and I used to go every year. Then we would make apple pie and apple crisp. My dad even made apple wine one year. That was gross!

Owen: I didn't know there was such a thing as apple wine.

Josie: Well, trust me, you aren't missing anything. What about you, Owen? What do you want to do with the money you made today?

Owen: I thought about buying a new video game. But I kind of like your idea, Josie. It would be fun to go apple picking in the fall. I've never done anything like that.

Maggie: I've never been apple picking either, Owen. I planned to spend any money I made doing something I've never done before...apple picking it is! Let me start counting...

Narrator: *Maggie takes a few minutes to add up how much each person has made. She finishes and puts down her notebook.*

Eddie: Well, how did you do, sis?

Maggie: Just a waffle iron, an old alarm clock, and a few other random things...for a whopping total of six dollars!

Owen: I guess it's six dollars more than you had before, right?

Maggie: Absolutely. Some of you made a lot more than six dollars!

Narrator: *Maggie reads each person's name and tells them how much money they have made so far.*

Tia: That's awesome!

Josie: If Owen, Maggie, and I go apple picking, would the rest of you want to come too?

Melvin: I'm in!

Eddie: Sure, why not? What about you, Emma?

Emma: Sure. I like hanging out with you guys.

Tia: Same! I'm in for apple picking. Steve, what about you?

Steve: I still want to buy lottery tickets with the money I make.

Josie: C'mon, Steve, we're all going!

Melvin: Yeah, c'mon, Steve.

Steve: I want to buy lottery tickets. How much does apple picking cost?

Josie: It depends on how many apples you want to pick. Well, it actually depends on the weight of the apples. You probably won't need more than ten dollars.

Maggie: What do you think, Steve? Can you save ten dollars between now and October?

Steve: I can do that.

Maggie: All right then. Do we all agree to save at least ten dollars to go apple picking this fall? It's not too far away.

Narrator: *Everyone agrees.*

Eddie: Well, that will be fun! And speaking of fun, I wonder if the rain has slowed down enough for us to reopen the sale.

Melvin: I think the rain is stopping.

Narrator: *Maggie turns on the TV to look at the weather radar.*

Maggie: Hmmm. Melvin is right; the rain is stopping for now. But it looks like we could get more rain later this afternoon.

Owen: I say we turn our *yard* sale into a *garage* sale and hope for the best.

Maggie: We may need to pull a couple tables out onto the driveway so people can move around in the garage, but I like what you're thinking, Owen.

Eddie: We have about two more hours until the end of the sale. Everyone ready?

Melvin: Let's do it!

Maggie: Remember, we decided to donate whatever we don't sell today. Is everyone still okay with that?

Narrator: *Everyone nods.*

Maggie: Eddie, you still okay with hauling the stuff in your truck?

Eddie: Yes, ma'am.

Maggie: Let's go try to squeeze out a few more apples!

Narrator: *Steve looks at Maggie with a confused look on his face.*

Maggie: I mean, let's go make more money! You can use your money for apple picking or lottery tickets or whatever you want.

Steve: Okay then, let's do it!

What Do You Think?

1. Have you ever heard the saying, "One person's trash is another person's treasure"? What does this mean?

2. Have you ever sold things at a yard sale? Did you make a "quick buck," or was it more work than you expected?

3. If you made an extra fifty dollars this weekend, what would you do with the money?

Play 2

What to Read Next

CHARACTERS

Owen	Steve
Emma	Josie
Tia	Melvin
Eddie	Narrator

<u>Act I</u>

<u>Narrator</u>: *This play takes place during a book club meeting at Java House. As the play begins, all the members are sitting at their usual table.*

<u>Owen</u>: Well, we're all here. Should we start reading?

<u>Steve</u>: Maggie and Eddie aren't here yet. Should we wait for them?

<u>Emma</u>: Oh, I forgot! Maggie has the flu. She won't be here tonight.

<u>Josie</u>: What about Eddie?

Emma: I don't know. Let me check my phone.

Narrator: *Emma opens her purse and pulls out her phone.*

Emma: Ah! Here's a text from Eddie. It says, "Hi Em. I will be late tonight. Start without me if you want to."

Narrator: *Owen opens his book and flips through the last few pages.*

Owen: We only have six pages to read. I bet we could finish before Eddie gets here.

Tia: Let's do it. It feels like we've been reading *The Time Machine* forever!

Melvin: I know! I'm ready to vote for our next book.

Emma: Oh, I forgot again!

Narrator: *Emma pulls an envelope out of her purse. She opens the envelope and unfolds a few pieces of paper. At the top of the first page is a picture of a book and the words "What to Read Next."*

Emma: Maggie dropped off the book list. She wrote a note on the top.

Narrator: *Josie leans over to read the note.*

Josie: Maggie says, "Have fun at book club, everyone! Since you will probably finish *The Time Machine* tonight, here is the list you can choose from for our next book. Happy voting!"

Tia: So, who's ready to start reading?

Steve: Aren't we going to wait on Eddie?

Tia: He said we could start without him.

Josie: Besides, we don't wait on anyone else when they're late.

Steve: That's true. I guess we could get started.

Tia: Is that okay with everyone else?

Narrator: *The members nod their heads and open their books to the very last chapter of the book. Owen reads one page. Melvin reads next, and Owen helps him with the words he doesn't know. After only ten minutes, the group finishes the book.*

Tia: Hmmm. That wasn't how I thought that story would end.

Owen: What did you think would happen?

Tia: I don't know, but I didn't think he would get back inside that machine!

Josie: Me neither! I wouldn't touch that thing.

Steve: If I could travel through time, I'd go to 1986 and watch the Bears win the Super Bowl. That would be awesome.

Owen: I'd go back to the time I saw the Rolling Stones in concert. Or maybe when I saw Springsteen.

Tia: You wouldn't want to go further back into the past? Or into the future?

Owen: No way! You saw how things turn out in the year...

Narrator: *Owen flips through the pages of the book and finds the year the Time Traveler went to.*

Owen: ...the year 802,701. No, thank you!

Narrator: *Everyone laughs*

Melvin: Time to vote for our next book! Emma, let's see that list.

Narrator: *Emma hands the list to Melvin. Owen leans over and looks at the list with Melvin.*

Steve: What's on the list?

Owen: Let's see...we have almost three pages of choices. But there's only one copy. Should I just read the list?

Melvin: Go for it, man.

Narrator: *Owen reads the list of book titles and the summaries after each title. A summary is a short description of a book*

Owen: All right, everyone, what do you think?

Steve: I vote for *The Hunger Games*. It's cool. I watched the movie at my cousin's.

Emma: What is *The Hunger Games* again?

Josie: It's a story that takes place very far in the future. But maybe not as far in the future as *The Time Machine*. Every year, a teenage boy and girl from twelve districts have to go into an arena and fight to the death. The last person alive is the winner. There's a pretty cool twist at the end, but I don't want to spoil it. What do you think, guys?

Emma: I think it sounds kinda scary.

Steve: Maybe a little. Katniss is hot, though.

Josie: Never mind that. Katniss is the main character. She's an archer, which means she uses a bow and arrow to shoot things...or people.

Owen: Sounds cool. Count me in for *The Hunger Games*.

Steve: Nice!

Tia: I saw parts of the movie on TV one night. It was too violent for me, so I turned the channel. Weren't there any other books that sounded interesting?

Melvin: I want to read the one with the superhero squirrel!

Tia: Oh, right! *Flora and Ulysses*! That sounded good. Can I see the list, Owen?

Narrator: *Owen passes the list to Tia. She finds* Flora and Ulysses *on the list.*

Tia: *Flora and Ulysses* looks like it will be funny too. Plus, the writer of this book is the same woman who wrote *Because of Winn-Dixie*. Remember how much we liked that book?

Emma: Oh, yeah! I loved that book.

Josie: I wasn't in the club when you all read that. Don't you guys want to read something that is a little more...grown-up?

Tia: I don't think violence makes a book more grown-up. I vote for *Flora and Ulysses*.

Melvin: Me too! A squirrel using a typewriter...that's funny!

Emma: It does sound funny. Plus, we just finished *The Time Machine*. That book was okay, but it was...

Tia: Dark?

Emma: Yeah, dark.

Steve: What do you mean by "dark"?

Tia: Gloomy and depressing. I thought *The Time Machine* was a little depressing.

Owen: I guess so, but it's just a story, right?

Tia: True. But wouldn't it be nice to switch things up and read something funny and happy?

Melvin: Funny and happy. Sounds like me!

Emma: I'm with Tia and Melvin. Let's read something that isn't so depressing.

Josie: It's just a book, Emma. It doesn't mean you have to be depressed when you read it. Plus, *The Hunger Games* is super popular. Tons of people have read it.

Steve: The movie is awesome! We could watch it together when we finish the book. What do you say, Owen? Movie night at your apartment?

Owen: Sure, why not?

Tia: Okay, wait a minute. Steve, Josie, and Owen want to read *The Hunger Games*. Emma, Melvin, and I want to read *Flora and Ulysses*. That's a tie. Three against three.

Owen: If Eddie was here, he could be the tie-breaker.

Melvin: What's that?

Owen: When a vote is tied, like this one, all you need is for one more person to vote. Then, the vote will be four against three and there's a winner.

Melvin: Cool, look who's here now!

Narrator: *Eddie walks quickly into Java House. He looks hurried and a little upset as he pulls up a chair and sits down with the club.*

Act II

Emma: Are you okay, Eddie? You're never late.

Eddie: I'm okay, thanks, Em. You're right, I don't like to be late. Sorry, everyone.

Emma: What happened?

Eddie: The shower in the upstairs bathroom is leaking, and now the ceiling above the kitchen sink looks like it's about to fall down. Nina is out of town, so I had to stick around to let the plumber in the house...and he was running late!

Owen: I thought you knew how to fix everything, Eddie.

Eddie: Everything but plumbing, Owen. Everything but plumbing.

Narrator: *Eddie looks around and doesn't see any books.*

Eddie: So, catch me up. Where are your books?

Melvin: We finished!

Eddie: Nice job, guys. How did you like *The Time Machine*?

Owen: I thought it was pretty cool. A little weird, but cool.

Emma: I thought it was depressing.

Eddie: Yeah, I agree with both of you. It was a cool story, but a bit depressing too. So, I guess it's time to vote for the next book?

Tia: We already have. Three of us want to read *The Hunger Games*, and three of us want to read *Flora and Ulysses*.

Eddie: So the vote is tied? What do you usually do if there's a tie?

Emma: We've never had a tie before, but Owen said you could be our tie-breaker.

Eddie: Oh yeah? Hmmm...

Narrator: *Eddie looks down for a moment, then looks up at the book club members and shakes his head.*

Eddie: Sorry, guys, but I don't think I should be your tie-breaker.

Emma: Why not?

Josie: Yeah, why not?

Eddie: Because I think you can settle this on your own.

Owen: I guess, but wouldn't it be easier if you just voted?

Eddie: Probably, Owen. It might be easier if I break the tie. But I am looking at six people who know how to run their own book club. You all finished the last book and voted for your next book without any help from Maggie or me. Isn't that great?

Tia: I guess it is! We haven't done this on our own before.

Narrator: *Tia smiles and Melvin gives her a fist bump.*

Eddie: It may not be easy or comfortable, but I believe you can talk this through and come to an agreement.

Emma: You do? How?

Eddie: Through something called negotiation. Negotiation is when two people or two groups want different things, so they have a conversation and come to an agreement. Usually, both sides need to compromise.

Steve: I know this one...a compromise is when both sides have to be flexible and give up something so they can have an agreement.

Eddie: Exactly, Steve.

Josie: Since when do you know how to compromise, Steve?

Steve: I know how to compromise. I think *you're* the one who has trouble with that.

Tia: C'mon, you guys. Please don't fight.

Josie: Tia's right. Remember the agreement Maggie helped us write when I joined book club? We leave "our past" in the past during book club meetings.

Steve: Yeah, all right.

Narrator: *Just then, the phone in Eddie's pocket starts to ring. Eddie looks at it.*

Eddie: I'm sorry, guys. This is the plumber. I better answer. Is everyone okay?

Narrator: *Eddie looks at Emma and the others. They nod their heads. Eddie steps outside to talk to the plumber on the phone.*

Melvin: So what are we doing?

Tia: We are going to talk to each other until we can agree on a book. Right?

Narrator: *Everyone but Steve nods. Steve takes out his phone and starts to scroll through it.*

Josie: Well, since Steve isn't going to be part of our discussion...

Narrator: *Steve is irritated with Josie and pretends not to hear her. He decides to pay attention to sports scores instead so that he will not lose his temper.*

Josie: The five of us will have to decide.

Emma: I don't know, guys. I don't want to argue.

Josie: Who said anything about arguing? We're going to talk, that's all.

Narrator: *Emma lowers her head. Tia notices that she looks uncomfortable.*

Tia: We can disagree with each other and still be respectful. Right, Melvin? We talked about this in one of our *People in Action* meetings.

Melvin: That's right. R-E-S-P-E-C-T, I'll show you what it means to me.

Narrator: *Emma still looks upset.*

Tia: What's upsetting you, Emma?

Emma: It's just that...well...Josie always wins. She always gets her way.

Josie: No I don't! You get your way, too!

Emma: No I don't. I let you have your way. I don't like fighting like you do.

Narrator: *At the sound of arguing, Owen quietly gets up and walks to a nearby table.*

Melvin: Where are you going, Owen?

Owen: I don't do conflict. It makes me nervous to hear people fighting. I'm going to sit over here and listen to music till you guys make a decision. I'll be cool with either book.

Narrator: *Owen sits down and puts on his headphones.*

Josie: We're not fighting!

Melvin: But you are yelling.

Josie: Fine, I will lower my voice. We are not fighting. We are going to have a conversation. That's all.

Tia: We do two things in a conversation. We talk AND we listen. Melvin, will you tell us again why you want to read *Flora and Ulysses*?

Melvin: It sounds funny! I like squirrels, too.

Tia: What about you, Steve? Why do you want to read *The Hunger Games*?

Narrator: *Steve does not hear Tia's question.*

Tia: Steve?

Steve: Huh?

Tia: Do you want to talk about our next book?

<u>Steve</u>: Huh? Sorry. Not really. I'm checking the scores.

<u>Narrator</u>: *Steve goes back to looking at sports on his phone.*

<u>Tia</u>: Moving on, I guess. Josie, why do you want to read *The Hunger Games*?

<u>Josie</u>: Like I said, it's a cool story. The main character is a strong teenage girl who kicks butt. Doesn't that sound better than a story about a squirrel, Emma?

Emma: No. I want to read about the squirrel. The book we just finished was depressing, and *The Hunger Games* sounds depressing, too. I want to read something more cheerful.

Melvin: Me too.

Josie: This isn't fair! No one on my side is saying anything. Owen is listening to music and Steve is looking at sports.

Tia: Is anyone willing to change their vote?

Narrator: *Emma, Melvin, and Josie shake their heads.*

Josie: What about you, Tia? Will you change your vote?

Tia: I don't think so.

Emma: Now what do we do?

Steve: You just pick a third book.

Josie: What? *Now* you're paying attention?

Emma: What do you mean, Steve?

Steve: I mean we pick another book. Not *The Hunger Games* and not *Flora and Ulysses*. It's the easiest way to solve a tie. It's how we do it in my family.

Narrator: *Josie, Emma, Melvin, and Tia think about Steve's suggestion for a few moments. Melvin shrugs his shoulders and looks at the others.*

Melvin: Why don't we try that?

Tia: Sounds fair to me. Emma? Josie?

Emma: Okay, I guess that's fair.

Josie: Fine. I have a question for Steve, though. Steve, if you had the solution, why in the world did you wait so long to speak up?!

Act III

Narrator: *Eddie walks back inside the Java House. He puts his phone in his pocket and rejoins the group.*

Eddie: Why did Nina and I buy such an old house?

Emma: You bought it because it is pretty and has lots of land, remember?

Eddie: Right. Well, this pretty old house seems to be falling apart! This is going to be an expensive repair. They have to tear out the ceiling in the kitchen...

Narrator: *Owen notices that Eddie has rejoined the group. He takes off his headphones and walks back to his seat.*

Melvin: Bummer, man.

Eddie: Yeah, it's a bummer for sure. So, what did you all decide about your next book?

Josie: We decided not to read either book.

Steve: It was my idea. When there is a tie in my family, we pick a third option. That way, nobody wins and nobody loses.

Eddie: Not bad, Steve. That could work. What do you all think?

Owen: Works for me. I'd rather us just get along.

Tia: But we can't get along all the time, Owen. We have to be able to disagree respectfully.

Owen: I know. Arguments just make me nervous.

Emma: Me too.

Tia: At *People in Action*, we learned that we should stand up for ourselves, even if we feel nervous or uncomfortable.

Eddie: That's great, Tia. Sounds like a cool group.

Melvin: It is. We learn how to talk about what we want and what we need.

Tia: Emma, do you want to check out a meeting with me and Melvin sometime?

Emma: Sure. When do you meet?

Tia: We meet on the third Thursday of the month at the main library. I can ask my dad if we can take you next month, if you want.

Emma: Okay, sure. Thanks, Tia!

Tia: Maybe I'll bring some information about *People in Action* for all of us to read?

Owen: It sounds nice, Tia, but the library is on the other side of town. I doubt I can walk there.

Tia: We talk about getting around town in our meetings. Transportation is tough for most of us.

Owen: Okay, well, maybe I will give it a try. I'll have to check out the bus routes.

Narrator: *Josie clears her throat.*

Josie: We only have ten minutes left. Can we decide on our next book?

Owen: Okay, we need to look at the list again.

Narrator: *Emma picks up the list and looks at the last page.*

Emma: We could read *Wonder*. Remember, Josie, we almost watched the movie *Wonder* a couple weeks ago.

Josie: Yeah. Then we watched that baking competition instead. Those cakes were amazing!

Emma: *You* wanted to watch the baking competition. I wanted to watch *Wonder*.

Narrator: *Eddie smiles at Emma and nods his head. This shows Emma that he is supporting her.*

Josie: Oh. I thought you wanted to watch the baking show, too.

Narrator: *Emma shakes her head no.*

Owen: I saw the movie *Wonder*. It's a pretty good flick. What do you guys think?

<u>Steve</u>: Oh yeah, Julia Roberts is in that movie. I'm in.

<u>Eddie</u>: Melvin? Tia? What do you think?

<u>Melvin</u>: Let's read *Wonder*.

<u>Tia</u>: I agree. Josie, are you okay with reading *Wonder* next?

<u>Josie</u>: Okay. I suppose I can read *The Hunger Games* on my own. We could all watch the movie at our apartment after we finish reading the book. Is that okay with you, Emma?

<u>Emma</u>: Sure! We could bake cookies for everyone. Or cupcakes with different kinds of frosting...

<u>Josie</u>: Or one of those fancy cakes we saw on TV.

<u>Narrator</u>: *Owen gets up and walks toward the counter at Java House.*

<u>Melvin</u>: Where are you going, Owen?

<u>Owen</u>: To buy a cookie! Emma and Josie are making me hungry!

What Do You Think?

1.   Conflict is another word for disagreement. Think about a time when you disagreed with someone. Was it easy to tell that person? Or maybe you chose not to say anything?

2.   Some of the members in this club belong to a group that helps them to advocate, or speak up, for themselves. Do you know any groups in your town like this? Are you a member of a group like this?

3.   In this story, half the club wanted to read a "darker," more serious book, and the other half wanted to read a "lighter," less serious book. Which do you prefer?

Play 3

Stay Calm, Help is on the Way

CHARACTERS

Melvin	Josie
Owen	Emma
Steve	Maggie
Delores Pickleford	Gavin Pickleford
Elevator Operator	Narrator

Act I, Scene I

Narrator: *This play takes place at a theater, before and after a symphony performance. As we begin the play, Emma, Josie, Steve, Owen, Melvin, and Maggie are walking down a short hallway toward the elevator.*

Melvin: Don't worry, guys. The second floor is better for listening to the symphony. My parents have season tickets. We come to the symphony all the time.

Josie: You must know a lot about the symphony.

Melvin: I know there are a lot of different musical instruments. They all play together and it makes beautiful music. There's a conductor, too. She's my favorite.

Narrator: *Melvin smiles and waves his arms like a conductor. The group arrives at the elevator and Melvin pushes the "up" button.*

Josie: Melvin, it was really nice of your parents to let us have these tickets.

Owen: And they bought three extra tickets so we could all come.

Emma: Well, not all of us. Eddie and Tia aren't here.

Steve: Don't you remember? Eddie said he couldn't come and Tia has to work.

Emma: I know *where* they are. I just wish they could be with us.

Maggie: I do, too, Emma. But how exciting is it that Tia has another DJ gig tonight? Her business seems to be doing well.

Owen: It's great. I'm really happy for her.

Emma: Yeah, me too.

Josie: This elevator is taking a long time to get here.

Steve: I know. I wonder where the stairs are. I don't like elevators anyway. I can just take the stairs.

Narrator: *Just then the elevator doors open. No one is inside.*

Melvin: Our ride is here!

Narrator: *The group enters the elevator. Melvin pushes the "2" button to go to the second floor. After a few seconds, the door closes.*

Maggie: I'm excited to see how the symphony and ballet tell the *Peter Pan* story! How long ago did we read *Peter Pan* in book club?

Steve: Last November.

Maggie: Well, all right then. You have a good memory, Steve!

Narrator: *The elevator reaches the second floor. After a few seconds, the doors open. Steve and Josie make eye contact as they exit the elevator. Josie smiles.*

Act I, Scene II

Narrator: *The performance is over. Club members are waiting in front of the elevator door on the second floor. Melvin pushes the "down" button.*

Emma: That was cool. I really liked how they did Tinkerbell!

Josie: I did too. I also liked the flying. That would be so fun!

Owen: You won't catch me doing that! Heights aren't my favorite.

Steve: Me neither.

Josie: Is this the world's slowest elevator?

Melvin: It is slow. Just have patience.

Narrator: *A moment later, the elevator door opens.*

The group steps into the elevator. As they wait for the door to close, an older woman (Delores Pickleford) and a young boy (Gavin Pickleford) walk quickly toward the elevator.

Delores: Hold the door, please!

Narrator: *Owen puts his hand on the edge of the open door so it won't close. The woman and the boy reach the elevator and step inside. Josie pushes the "1" button for the first floor.*

Delores: Thank you.

Owen: You're welcome.

Narrator: *The elevator doors close. After a couple seconds, the elevator begins to slowly move downward.*

Delores: This elevator is dreadfully slow. I do wish they would fix it.

Gavin: Nana, you say that every time we get on this elevator.

Delores: Yes, well. I believe I will speak with the theater manager again after we pick up our coats.

Narrator: *Maggie looks at Emma and makes a silly face. Emma laughs quietly. The elevator slows to a stop at the first floor. A few seconds pass. Everyone is waiting for the doors to open. A few more seconds pass. Josie pushes the "open door" button. The doors do not open.*

Act II

Steve: Oh no.

Melvin: It's okay, everybody. The elevator is just slow.

Narrator: *A few more seconds pass. The elevator doors remain closed.*

Emma: Should we press the emergency button?

Delores: Yes, I believe we've waited long enough.

Narrator: *Delores moves through the group toward the emergency button and speaker. She presses the button. Right away, everyone hears the sound of a ringing phone through the speaker.*

As it rings, the red light flashes. After two rings, an operator answers the phone and the red light stops flashing.

Operator: Operator. How may I help you?

Delores: Yes, hello. This is Mrs. Delores Pickleford. Our elevator doors have not opened. We arrived on the first floor at the Thornville Theater at least thirty seconds ago and the doors have not opened.

Operator: You said your elevator is no longer moving, but the doors have not opened?

Delores: Yes, that's exactly right. Will you open the doors, please?

Operator: I'm working on that. You said you're at the Thornville Theater?

Dolores: Yes, the Thornville Theater on Third Avenue.

Operator: Thornville Theater on Third?

Delores: Yes, that is right. The symphony just finished a performance.

Operator: The symphony just finished a performance?

Delores: Yes! Why do you keep repeating me? Can you open the door?

Operator: I understand you are frustrated, ma'am. Unfortunately, I'm not able to open the elevator door from here. I have sent EMTs from Third Avenue Station to your location. I'm going to stay on the line with you until they arrive, okay. Stay calm. Help is on the way.

Delores: All right, we'll try. Please do ask them to hurry.

Owen: Why don't we try knocking on the door? Someone in the lobby might hear us and be able to open the doors.

Operator: Hi, there. Sir, I don't know if I heard you correctly, but it is safer to wait for help to arrive, okay?

Owen: Okay, you got it.

Maggie: I don't have a cell phone signal. Does anyone else?

Narrator: *Emma, Josie, Owen, and Melvin look at their phones then shake their heads because their phones are not working in the elevator either. Josie looks at Steve. His face is pale.*

Josie: Steve, are you okay? Here, why don't you sit down?

Narrator: *Others move out of the way as Steve holds onto the handrail and slowly lowers himself to the floor.*

Delores: Oh my heavens, what next? Now someone is getting sick? Will the drama never end?

Josie: Ma'am, he doesn't feel well. This is a very overwhelming situation for him.

Steve: It's okay. I'm okay.

Narrator: *Josie bends down to look at Steve's face.*

Josie: Are you sure? If you think you might pass out, put your head between your knees.

Owen: That's right. I have to do that sometimes because of my head.

Gavin: What's wrong with your head?

Delores: Gavin, we do not ask people questions like that! It's not proper.

Owen: It's okay. I don't mind. When I was a very young man, I was on a bicycle and got hit by a car. My head hit the ground, and I got a brain injury. Now some things are hard for me to do and I get headaches and dizzy spells. That's how I know about putting your head between your legs.

Delores: I'm very sorry to hear that, sir. Gavin, leave this poor man alone now.

Narrator: *Josie hands Steve a tissue from her purse so he can wipe sweat from his face.*

Maggie: Hey, Steve. You doing okay?

Steve: I want off this elevator.

Maggie: I hear you, friend. If it helps, I don't think it will take long for the EMTs to get here. The Third Avenue fire station is just down the road.

Narrator: *Steve nods his head.*

Josie: Steve, you know what I was thinking about the other day? The tornado drill at the warehouse when we all got stuck in the tiny copy machine room. I don't know how we missed the "all clear" signal. Then Wanda came in to make copies. She was so surprised to see us she dropped all her papers! Ha!

Steve: Yeah, that was funny.

Melvin: Hey everyone, what do you do if you get tired of fast food?

Emma: What?

Melvin: Tell it to slow down.

Narrator: *Emma, Maggie, Owen, and Gavin chuckle.*

Melvin: I have another one. Why couldn't the skeleton fart in front of anyone?

Gavin: Why?

Melvin: He didn't have the guts.

Gavin: Ha! Good one. I have got a joke, too. What happened to the man who only ate Skittles?

Melvin: What?

Gavin: He farted rainbows.

Narrator: *Nearly everyone laughs a little bit. Melvin and Owen laugh a bit harder.*

Delores: That's enough of these nasty jokes. Can we have some peace and quiet, please?

Melvin: I'm sorry, I'll be quiet.

Gavin: And I'll be peace.

Narrator: *Everyone laughs this time, even Steve. Of course, Delores does not laugh. She shakes her head and places her hand on Gavin's shoulder.*

Josie: You're looking a little better, Steve.

Maggie: I think you're right, Josie.

Steve: I'm starting to feel a little better.

Operator: Hello, everyone. The EMTs have arrived at the theater. They should be there any moment.

Delores: Excellent, thank you.

Narrator: *Within a few moments, the EMTs knock on the elevator door. An EMT shouts to the people inside, asking them to stand as far away from the doors as possible. The EMTs use special tools to pry open the elevator doors. At last, the doors open.*

Act III

Narrator: *The group steps out of the elevator. Delores Pickleford and her grandson Gavin walk out first, then Steve and Josie, then the others. A small crowd has formed behind the EMTs, and they cheer and clap as everyone gets off the elevator.*

Melvin: Hey, guys, we're famous now!

Maggie: I think those people are just happy we are okay.

Josie: I'm just glad to be off that elevator!

Steve: So am I. My parents are picking me up. I better find them.

Josie: Yes, you should. They might be worried when they see the ambulance outside.

Steve: Right. Well, I'm going now, everyone.

Maggie: Steve, how about if someone walks with you till you find your parents' car?

Josie: I'll do it. Emma, I see Sonya waiting for us over by the concession stand. Will you tell her that I'm helping Steve and I'll be right back?

Narrator: *Steve and Josie walk outside to the parking lot to find Steve's parents. Emma walks over to their staff person, Sonya, to tell her that they need a few more minutes, then she returns to the group.*

Emma: How is everyone else getting home?

Maggie: Melvin, isn't that your staff person Gil standing by the door?

Melvin: Yep, that's him. Wait till I tell him this story! He's going to crack up.

Emma: What about Owen?

Maggie: Owen rode with me tonight. Are you ready to go home, Owen?

Owen: You bet. I'm tired.

Narrator: *Owen looks at his watch.*

Owen: It's almost 11:00 p.m.! No wonder I'm tired!

Narrator: *Gil walks closer to the group, and Melvin realizes it is time for him to leave.*

Melvin: I'm happy we all got to come to the symphony together. Now, put a smile on your face and keep it there till I see you at book club on Wednesday!

Narrator: *Melvin and the group say goodbye to one another. Josie walks back inside the lobby with a smile on her face.*

Maggie: Well, hello there. Thank you for taking such good care of Steve tonight. I'm sure he appreciated it, too.

Emma: Yeah, I haven't seen you guys be that nice to each other ever.

Josie: It was the right thing to do. I know about Steve's fear of elevators.

Maggie: It was also the *kind* thing to do.

Josie: I guess you're right. Steve said, "Thank you," and asked me if he could give me a hug before he got into his parents' car. That was nice.

Narrator: *Josie, Emma, and Maggie all smile at one another. Owen notices a commotion near the coat check.*

Owen: Hey, check that out!

Narrator: *In the corner of the theater lobby, Delores Pickleford is talking to the manager. She points her finger at him, then she points in the direction of the elevator. The manager hangs his head and nods.*

Owen: I'm glad I'm not that guy!

Emma: No doubt! She was not a nice lady.

Maggie: But her grandson sure is a funny little guy.

Narrator: *From behind Mrs. Pickleford's fur coat, Gavin Pickleford is making goofy faces at his new friends from the elevator. Owen waves at him.*

Owen: Goodnight, little dude!

Gavin: Goodnight, big dude!

What Do You Think?

1.   Lots of people are afraid of things like heights or being in cramped spaces. Is there anything you're really afraid of? What can you do to calm yourself if you are feeling afraid?

2.   Have you ever been to a symphony or ballet performance? What did you think of it?

3.   Gavin's grandmother is a very proper and formal person. Did you get to know any of your grandparents? What are/were they like?

Play 4

I Picked This One for You

CHARACTERS

Melvin

Emma

Josie

Owen

Narrator

Maggie

Tia

Steve

Eddie

<u>Act I</u>

<u>Narrator</u>: *This play takes place at an apple orchard in the fall. It is a bright sunny day with a clear blue sky. The book club members have gone apple picking, just as they said they would after their yard sale. Instead of walking around in one big group, they decide to split into teams of two people. Act I begins after everyone gets a bushel basket that they will fill with apples. They divide into pairs and head into the apple orchard.*

Melvin: Okay, Maggie, we're going to pick the best apples on this whole farm.

Maggie: We are? How will we know they're the best apples?

Melvin: That's easy; because we picked them!

Maggie: Hmm. All right, I can go along with that! Oh, wow, look at these big apples over here!

Narrator: *Melvin walks over to where Maggie is standing and looks up.*

Melvin: Perfect! Hey, Maggie, what kind of apple isn't an apple?

Maggie: What kind?

Melvin: A pineapple!

Maggie: Ha! Funny *and* true.

Narrator: *Melvin and Maggie begin choosing apples from the tree. To pick the apple, they grab it, give it a twist, and pull lightly. Then they add the apples to their basket and keep going.*

Maggie: Hey, Melvin, can I ask you a question?

Melvin: Sure!

Maggie: It is about something personal. So, if this is private and you don't want to talk about it, you don't have to. Okay?

Melvin: Okay.

Maggie: You don't have any brothers or sisters, right?

Melvin: Right. It's just me and my mom and dad.

Maggie: I know this isn't a happy thing to think about, but I wonder...have you and your mom and dad talked about where you will live when they pass away?

Melvin: You mean when they die?

Maggie: Yes.

Melvin: Oh yeah. When I turned thirty, we had a family meeting about it. My parents said we needed a plan so I would know what to do...and stuff. Then they showed me where they keep a big yellow folder with all their important papers.

Maggie: It's really good to hear that you and your parents have already talked about this. So, what did you all decide?

Melvin: About what?

Maggie: About where you want to live.

Melvin: Oh, right. I'm going to look for a roommate to live with me.

Narrator: *Melvin and Maggie continue to pick apples as they talk.*

Maggie: Are you going to stay at your house where you live now, or will you move?

Melvin: I'm staying at home. I love my house. Mom and Dad said it will be paid off soon, so I won't have to pay a lot to live there. We talked about other things, but I don't remember it all. They said the most important thing to remember when the time comes is to call their lawyer, Mr. Collins. They wrote his name and phone number on the front of the big yellow folder.

Maggie: It's really good you have all that info, Mel. So, how do you feel about living with someone other than your parents someday?

Narrator: *Melvin looks up into the sky and then down at the ground. Then he shrugs his shoulders.*

Melvin: I don't know.

Maggie: I'm sorry. I know this isn't fun to think about, but I appreciate you sharing with me.

Melvin: My mom says I'm too social to live by myself. She says I'm going to need a roommate.

Maggie: Do you agree with her?

Melvin: Yeah, I guess. I love talking and joking with people. I'm going to find a super cool roommate, too.

Maggie: I bet you will!

Melvin: Oh! The other important thing I'm supposed to remember is that it is my choice to live where I want. And I can change my mind if I want to.

Maggie: That's exactly what my parents told Emma.

Melvin: That sounds good.

Maggie: It is. But...

Narrator: *Maggie looks closely at the apple in her hand. She looks for any bruises or marks. She decides to put it in her basket.*

Maggie: We had a big family meeting last week, probably like the one you and your parents had. My parents, Emma, Eddie, and I were all there.

Melvin: Where are your parents? Do they live here?

Maggie: No, they moved to Arizona when they retired. They love it there.

Melvin: I've been to Arizona! We went to the Grand Canyon. Did you go to the Grand Canyon when you went to see your parents?

Maggie: Well, we had this family meeting over the computer. We sat in front of our computers and we could see each other and hear each other. Anyway, I guess I'm wondering what Emma will decide. She doesn't need to decide right away, but I hope she decides to come live with me someday.

Melvin: You do? But she lives with Josie.

Maggie: That's true. But as we get older, I think it would be good for Emma and me to live together so we can help take care of each other. Does that make sense?

Narrator: *Melvin nods his head.*

Melvin: It is Emma's choice. Emma and Tia and I learned more about making choices in our *People in Action* meeting last week.

Narrator: *Melvin picks an apple to put in his basket. Then he changes his mind and takes a big bite out of the apple instead. Maggie smiles.*

Maggie: Good idea! I'm hungry, too.

Narrator: *Maggie takes an apple from her basket and bites into it.*

Maggie: Thank you for talking about this with me, Melvin. Emma knows I want her to live with me. Eddie wants her to live with him too! I just wonder what she's thinking.

Melvin: Did I help you?

Maggie: You did. Thanks, Melvin. Since the family meeting last week, I've been pushing Emma a little bit. I want her to make a choice, and I want her to choose to live with me. But, you're right. This is her choice to make when she is ready.

Melvin: Her life, her choice!

Narrator: *Maggie nods her head and gives Melvin a fist bump.*

Melvin: Look at *this* apple! I bet this is the biggest apple on the planet!

Narrator: *Melvin tells Maggie a few of his new jokes as they continue to pick apples. As usual, Melvin laughs at his own jokes, and this makes Maggie laugh. Maggie has a loud and goofy-sounding laugh.*

Act II

Narrator: *Owen and Eddie are picking apples a couple rows over from Maggie and Melvin. Eddie chuckles quietly when he hears the sound of Maggie's goofy laugh.*

Eddie: I'd know *that* laugh anywhere.

Owen: That's Maggie, right?

Eddie: Definitely.

Narrator: *Maggie laughs again, even louder. This time, Eddie and Owen start laughing, too.*

Owen: Beautiful day, isn't it?

Eddie: Gorgeous! Fall is the best season of the year.

Owen: I agree. Summer is too hot, and winter is too cold. Fall is just right.

Eddie: What about spring?

Owen: Oh, I sneeze all the way through spring.

Eddie: Emma and I have spring allergies, too.

Owen: It must be nice to live so close to your sisters.

Eddie: It is. What about you, Owen? Do you have family nearby?

Owen: After my parents passed away, my older sister moved to Florida. That was about twenty years ago. I only have one cousin, and he lives in Kansas, I think.

Eddie: Do you and your sister keep in touch?

Owen: No, not really. Both of my nieces moved out, had kids, and moved back in with my sister. So, she's pretty busy.

Eddie: Well, I feel sorry for your sister and nieces. They don't know what a great guy they're missing.

Narrator: *Eddie and Owen are picking apples from trees next to each other. Eddie looks over at Owen and notices a smile on his face.*

Eddie: My wife Nina and I moved back to town so we could be close to our families. It's been great. Well, not *all* great. There's that money pit we call a house we're fixing up. There's always something to fix or rebuild in that house.

Owen: Sorry about that, man. At least I get to see you and Nina when I'm at work at the hardware store!

Eddie: Ha! It feels like I'm there every day!

Owen: I *am* there every day—well, almost. Anyway, Maggie and Emma sure were excited for you to move back home.

Eddie: That's good to hear. Actually, we just had a family meeting. It's funny; we were all on our own computers. Who would have thought you could have a family meeting with nobody in the same room?

Owen: Not me! Even your parents were there?

Eddie: Yep, all the way from their computer in Arizona. They want Emma to think about where she wants to live when they pass away. I don't know if she's ready to make that decision, but Nina and I would love for her to come stay with us.

Owen: Wow. You're lucky to have each other.

Eddie: We are. What about you, Owen?

Owen: What's that?

Eddie: Well, sometimes we have friends that feel like family. Is there anyone in your life like that?

Owen: Oh, I see. Yeah, I have a good buddy at work. Plus friends from my apartment complex. We've all lived there for years. I guess you could say they feel like family. One guy and I talked about moving into a two-bedroom place to save money.

Eddie: What happened?

Owen: Both of us realized that we didn't want a roommate. I like having my own space.

Eddie: I hear you, man. After being in the Marines for twenty years, I don't want to share space with anyone but Nina and Emma...if she decides to live with us.

Narrator: *Owen picks an apple and notices a worm hole in it. He shows it to Eddie who jokes about using it to prank Maggie. The men chuckle.*

Eddie: That's great, Owen. It sounds like you've got your people.

Narrator: *Owen nods his head.*

Owen: Plus, my high school English teacher, Mrs. Winkle, still checks in on me. She's a sweet lady. Actually, I met Maggie at Mrs. Winkle's retirement party. I forget, what does Maggie teach?

Eddie: Spanish.

Owen: That's right, Spanish. Anyway, I was talking to Maggie at Mrs. Winkle's party. She told me about the book club and invited me to join. Here I am!

Eddie: I'm so glad you're here. I know I haven't been a part of the book club as long as you have, but it seems like everybody cares a lot for each other.

Owen: That's true. I suppose I also think of my book club friends like family, too.

Eddie: Good! Here, catch, brother!

Narrator: *Eddie tosses an apple to Owen. Owen catches it and throws one of his apples to Eddie. Eddie tries to catch it with one hand, but it falls and rolls into the aisle in between the rows of apple trees. He walks to pick it up and sees Steve and Josie.*

Eddie: Hi, guys! How's it going?

Narrator: *Steve and Josie say, "Good" at the same time.*

Eddie: Great. See you in a little while!

Narrator: *Eddie walks back to the tree where Owen is standing, and the two men continue to fill their baskets with apples.*

Act III

Narrator: *Josie and Steve decide to walk down a row of apple trees where there are no other people.*

Josie: Beautiful day, isn't it?

Steve: It is. My mom calls it "sweater weather" because it's cool enough for a sweater, but not cold enough for a coat.

Josie: Sweater weather? I've never heard that before. I like wearing sweaters. This is one of my favorites.

Narrator: *Josie holds her arms open so Steve can admire her sweater.*

Steve: It's pretty. It looks comfortable, too.

Josie: It is. It is nice to wear things that don't smell like Big Jim's Barbeque!

Steve: I would love that smell. Not you, though!

Josie: No, it's not my favorite part of the job.

Narrator: *Steve and Josie are picking apples from the same tree. Josie is choosing her apples very carefully. Steve is paying more attention to Josie than he is the apples.*

Josie: Oh! I forgot to tell you the best news!

Steve: What's that?

Josie: You know my super mean boss, Sadie?

Steve: The super bossy boss?

Josie: Yes. Well, guess what! She got married to a man who lives in New Orleans, and she's moving there. No more Sadie!

Steve: That's good news!

Josie: We're all pretty excited about it, but we don't talk about it when Sadie is at work. It's funny; she acts like she's sad to leave, but I don't think *she* likes *us* either. Her last day is next week, thank goodness.

Steve: That's great.

Narrator: *Josie picks a couple more apples and puts them in her basket.*

Josie: I can't wait to make apple crisp with all these apples. I got my mom's recipe yesterday. Can you believe my mom and Aunt Trudy are already planning their holiday baking?

Steve: Does your Aunt Trudy still have that big German shepherd? His name is Duke, right?

Narrator: *Josie is surprised. She looks at Steve and smiles.*

Josie: Yeah, Duke...I can't believe you remember that! You only met my Aunt Trudy once, when we first started dating.

Steve: I remember everything from when we dated. Your mom was mad about all the dog fur from Duke.

Josie: Oh, that's right. Aunt Trudy let Duke get up on the couch. We found dog fur on that couch for weeks. It's really not nice to let your dog on other people's furniture.

Steve: I guess not.

Narrator: *Steve and Josie are quiet for a few moments.*

Steve: I hope I get to try your apple crisp.

Josie: Sure you can. Maybe Emma and I will have a party. An apple-themed party!

Steve: I've never been to a party with an apple theme before.

Josie: I can't wait to talk to Emma about it. Everyone can bring something they made with all their apples to share. I wonder if anyone knows how to make pie crust. I love apple pie...

Narrator: *Josie is still talking when Steve walks over to a nearby tree. He looks around for the prettiest apple he can find. He picks it and walks over to Josie.*

Josie: Were you listening, Steve? I was talking about the party.

Steve: I heard you.

Narrator: *Steve holds up the pretty apple for Josie.*

Steve: Here. I picked this one for you. Maybe you can put it in your apple crisp.

Josie: How...sweet. Thank you, Steve. It's almost too pretty to eat.

Narrator: *Josie leans over and kisses Steve on the cheek. They stay close and stare at each other for a few seconds. Just as they are about to kiss again, they hear Tia say, "Hi, guys!"*

Act IV

Narrator: *Tia and Emma have just turned a corner when they find Steve and Josie standing very close to each other. After they say "hi" to each other, Tia and Emma walk quickly to a different row of trees.*

Tia: Are you thinking what I'm thinking?

Emma: I think so. Were they kissing?

Tia: I don't know, but it looked like they were going to.

Narrator: *Emma and Tia giggle a little bit.*

Emma: I do feel bad for interrupting.

Tia: Well, they are in a public place, so they can't expect total privacy. But I know what you mean. Do you think they might get back together?

Emma: I don't know. Josie talked about Steve a couple times since we went to the symphony. I wonder if she likes him again.

Tia: I wonder too. I can't tell with Steve, but Josie does seem more cheerful lately.

Emma: Oh boy, I can't wait to tell Maggie.

Narrator: *Tia and Emma choose a tree and begin picking the last apples that will fill their baskets.*

Emma: Or maybe I shouldn't say anything. I don't think Josie would want me to.

Tia: You're a good friend, Emma. And you're probably right. We should let Josie and Steve talk about it if they want to. I'm going to be so curious, though!

Emma: I know!

Tia: Sometimes I wish *I* had a boyfriend.

Emma: Yeah, me too. I've never had a boyfriend.

Tia: I haven't had a boyfriend since high school. My parents tell me not to worry about it. They tell me that I'll meet someone when the time is right.

Emma: My parents say that, too!

Tia: Easy for them to say, right? They already found someone!

Emma: Right!

Tia: Well, I'm happy for Josie and Steve...if they're happy.

Narrator: *Emma nods her head and the women continue to pick apples. Tia bends down and picks up her basket with her right hand.*

Tia: My basket is so heavy! I think I'm almost finished. How about you?

Emma: Yeah, my basket is almost full. Tia, do you remember when I said I talked to my mom and dad and Maggie and Eddie over the computer last week?

Narrator: *Tia nods her head yes.*

Emma: Well... It's just... I'm nervous.

Tia: Nervous? What are you nervous about?

Emma: My mom and dad want me to think about what I want to do after...after they die. They want me to think about where I want to live. They help pay for my apartment now. But they think I should live with Maggie or Eddie. Not now. But, you know, someday. I'm supposed to make a choice.

Tia: Oh wow. What are you going to do?

Emma: I don't know, Tia. I love my family. But I'm happy in my apartment. What would you do?

Tia: I like living at home with my mom and dad. I know they won't live forever, though. My sister in Dallas says I can come live with her. It would be great to be with my nieces and nephew.

My cousin in Atlanta wants me to live with her, too. Plus, my Aunt Patricia and Uncle Julio live here; they always tell me I can live with them. I guess I have a lot of options when the time comes.

Emma: Haven't you ever wanted to live on your own? *Not* with family?

Tia: No, I hope I can always live with family. But that's what is right for me. You have to decide what is right for you. Just like we talked about in *People in Action*.

Emma: That's right. My life, my choice!

Tia: You got it, girl!

Narrator: *Emma smiles at Tia.*

Emma: The thing is...I mean...I don't think I want to live with Maggie *or* Eddie. I like living on my own. I like having a roommate. I know Josie can be bossy, but she's not so bad. She's also thoughtful and fun sometimes.

Tia: It sounds like you know what you want to do.

Emma: Yeah.

Narrator: *Tia waits patiently for Emma to say more.*

Emma: I don't want to hurt their feelings.

Tia: Maggie and Eddie? You don't want to hurt their feelings?

Emma: Uh-huh. I know they both want me to live with them. I love them and I'm so glad they are here. But I don't want to live with them again. They drove me nuts when we were growing up!

Tia: Emma, I think you should just be honest with Maggie and Eddie.

Emma: You do?

Tia: For sure. They're going to love you no matter what you decide! I think they will be proud of you for wanting to be independent.

Emma: Yeah, maybe. But what if I change my mind someday and decide I do want to live with one of them but it's too late?

Tia: You are allowed to change your mind. Maggie and Eddie will understand.

Emma: Thanks, Tia. This helps. I've been so worried about hurting their feelings.

<u>Tia</u>: I think Eddie and Maggie just want you to be happy.

<u>Emma</u>: Yeah. You're right. I'll tell them. Not today, though.

<u>Narrator</u>: *Tia and Emma pick up their baskets full of apples and start walking back toward the club's meeting spot.*

<u>Emma</u>: Good grief, we have a lot of apples to eat!

<u>Tia</u>: This basket is too heavy! I might need to take a break. It's hurting my hand.

Emma: Let me carry it, Tia. I can carry both of our baskets.

Tia: Are you sure?

Emma: Yep. I'm very strong. I carry a lot of things at work.

Tia: Okay, thanks. That's a big help.

Narrator: *Tia sets her basket down on the ground with a thump. Emma bends down and grabs the handle of Tia's basket with her left hand. She carries her basket in her right hand. She looks at all the apples.*

Emma: Josie should have plenty of apples to make apple crisp.

Tia: Apple crisp, apple pie, apple turnovers, apple cinnamon muffins, apple tarts...

Emma: I know! Josie and I can have an apple dessert party.

Tia: I'll bring the music!

Narrator: *Tia and Emma are the last pair to join the group at the meeting spot. Everyone looks a little tired but very happy.*

What Do You Think?

1.   Who is in your family? Is there anyone in your life who isn't related to you but *feels* like family?

2.   Are you living where you want to live? If not, where would you like to live? Would you like to live with other people or by yourself?

3.   Steve and Josie seem to like each other again. Do you think they should get back together? Have you ever changed your mind about an old boyfriend or girlfriend?

4.   What is your favorite season of the year?

Play 5

Nell Ferris and the Readers

CHARACTERS

Maggie	Nell Ferris
Emma	Steve
Owen	Eddie
Melvin	Tia
Josie	Narrator

Act I, Scene I

Narrator: *This play starts at the end of Maggie's Tuesday night creative writing class. On this night, Maggie and her classmates had a guest teacher, Nell Ferris. Nell is a famous writer from London, England. She is known for writing romance and mystery books. After the class ends, Maggie stays behind to chat with Nell.*

Maggie: Hi there! Thank you so much. This was so helpful. I took five pages of notes!

Nell: Oh, brilliant. I'm so glad.

Maggie: I can't wait to rewrite the romance scenes in my story with your tips. I also think I can use the activity we did at the beginning of class with my book club.

Nell: Is this the book club you mentioned during class? Is it a book club or a writing club?

Maggie: I suppose it's whatever we want it to be! We usually read together, but sometimes we like to try other things. We've written poetry, letters to family members, and a couple short stories. Some of the members, like my sister Emma, need help reading or writing. So we all help each other.

Nell: I love the idea of including everyone, no matter what. I had an aunt who would have loved this kind of group. May I ask your name?

Maggie: Of course! I'm Maggie. It's so nice to meet you.

Narrator: *Maggie and Nell shake hands.*

Nell: I would love to hear more about your book club, if you don't mind?

Maggie: Sure! There are eight of us, including my twin brother and me. My brother and I volunteer as group facilitators, but it usually feels more like hanging out with my sibs and friends than volunteering. We meet at a coffee shop a couple blocks from here once a week to read and hang out.

We've read everything from *A Wrinkle in Time* to *Holes* to *Charlotte's Web*.

<u>Nell</u>: Brilliant. Perhaps the next time I'm in town I could visit your book club?

<u>Maggie</u>: That would be wonderful. Or, if you're still in town tomorrow night, that's when we meet. I think everyone would be excited to have a *real* writer visit!

<u>Nell</u>: If you write, you're a real writer.

<u>Maggie</u>: I suppose, but you know what I mean. You actually make money writing books!

<u>Nell</u>: That's true. But it took a while. I think I have a rejection letter from every publisher in the U.S. and in the U.K.!

Maggie: I, for one, am glad you didn't give up!

Nell: So am I! Now back to your book club...my flight doesn't leave till Thursday morning. I'd love to visit your group tomorrow night if that would be okay?

Maggie: That would be awesome! We meet from 7:00–8:00 p.m. at a coffee shop called Java House.

Narrator: *Nell takes her cell phone out of her briefcase and enters the info from Maggie.*

Nell: Okay, brilliant. I'll be there.

Maggie: This is so exciting! I pick up my sister from work when I leave here. I can't wait to tell her.

Narrator: *Nell smiles, then she and Maggie say goodbye to each other.*

Act I, Scene II

Narrator: *Maggie drives up to the front door of the rec center where Emma works. It is cold and snowy outside, so Emma rushes to get inside Maggie's car.*

Maggie: Hey, sis. How was work?

Emma: Today was boring. Hardly anyone came to the rec center tonight.

Maggie: Yeah, most people don't like to go out in the snow if they don't have to. I noticed the holiday lights are up in the lobby. Do you get to decorate the big desk where you sit?

Emma: There are lights everywhere! It's nice. I also brought in one of my snowmen from home to put on the big desk. Everyone likes his big floppy hat. But I'm leaving the rest of my decorations at home so Josie and I can have them for the New Year's Eve party.

Maggie: Good plan, Em. I have some fun news.

Emma: Okay.

Maggie: We had a guest teacher at my creative writing class tonight. Have you ever heard of Nell Ferris?

Narrator: *Emma shakes her head no.*

Maggie: She's a famous writer. Well, maybe not that famous. She writes books that are mysteries and romance, all wrapped up in the same story. They call that a "genre bender." Anyway, I was talking to her after class and ended up inviting her to visit our book club tomorrow night. Is that okay with you?

Emma: Uh-huh.

Maggie: Wait till you meet her, Em. She is older than us but younger than Mom. She's from London and says "brilliant" all the time. What do you think?

Emma: I like the mystery part. I wonder if she's read all the *Nancy Drew* books like I have.

Maggie: You can ask her tomorrow night!

Emma: We won't have to write kissy romance stuff, will we?

Maggie: I don't know, sis. We'll have to wait to find out!

Act II

Narrator: *It is the next evening at Java House. Tia has not yet arrived for book club. Nell Ferris has not arrived either. Steve looks at his phone to find out what time it is. It is 7:04.*

Steve: Tia is late. It's 7:04.

Owen: Yeah, Tia is almost never late.

Steve: It's 7:05 now.

Maggie: Things come up sometimes, you know?

Steve: Yeah, like last week when Josie had to work late at Big Jim's. Or like your broken plumbing, Eddie.

Eddie: Ugh, don't remind me!

Maggie: Well, while we wait for Tia, I have some fun news for our meeting tonight.

Narrator: *Just then, Tia walks into Java House. She looks upset.*

Maggie: Hi, Tia! I was just about to tell everyone about some fun news.

Melvin: Hi, Tia!

Tia: Hi, Melvin. Hi, everyone. I'm sorry I'm late. I was on the phone. I need a few minutes to calm down. I'm really upset.

Emma: What happened, Tia?

Tia: I didn't get the gig.

Emma: Oh no. I'm so sorry.

Melvin: What gig?

Tia: A wedding next summer. It was going to be my first time DJ'ing a wedding. I'm disappointed...and...and...frustrated!

Narrator: *Tia lifts her hands to her face and begins to cry quietly.*

Owen: I'm really sorry, Tia.

Emma: Me too. What happened? You and the bride had a good meeting, right?

Tia: We did! I thought it was great! But I guess she had an even better meeting with Spencer.

Josie: Wait, who is Spencer?

Tia: He's another DJ. *Spencer's Party Machine*. One of my competitors.

Owen: Hmmm. I like your name much better. *Tia's Tunes* has a nice ring to it.

Tia: Thank you, Owen.

Emma: Would you like a hug?

Tia: Thanks, Emma, I'm okay, though. I feel more angry than sad. It's not even Spencer's fault.

Josie: Whose fault is it? The bride's?

Tia: I don't know. I...well...a wedding DJ usually has to make a lot of announcements at the reception. Spencer has a really nice speaking voice. And I sound like—I sound like me. CP screwed up my speech. I hate it.

Narrator: *Tia covers her face with her hands and begins to cry again. Then she takes a tissue out of her purse to wipe her tears and dab at her nose.*

Josie: She can't turn you down just because you have a disability. That's illegal.

Emma: That's right. It's discrimination!

Steve: Did the bride say she wasn't picking you because of your voice?

Tia: No. All she said is, "It was a really tough choice." I guess I just can't help but wonder. Spencer has the voice of a radio DJ. But his prices are so high. Oh, well. Sorry for crying, everyone.

Maggie: You don't need to apologize, Tia. You are allowed to cry. You're with friends.

Owen: Before my accident, I was a drummer in a band. We weren't professionals like you, Tia. But, man, it was tough to get gigs. We would think we had a gig in the bag, but then we'd find out that another band got the job. We were disappointed *a lot*.

Eddie: I didn't know you used to be in a band, Owen! Cool. It sounds like it wasn't always easy, though.

Owen: No. Sometimes it sucked.

Melvin: Yeah. This sucks.

Narrator: *Melvin notices Nell approaching the table. Others turn their heads to look where Melvin is looking.*

Melvin: Hello!

Nell: Greetings, everyone! I'm Nell. Maggie said you wouldn't mind if I joined you tonight. Is that okay? Actually, before you say anything, let me excuse myself and find the restroom. That will give you time to decide together.

Act III, Scene I

Narrator: *While Nell is in the restroom, Tia begins to feel better. Maggie tells the group about Nell, and they decide they would like her to stay for the meeting. When Nell returns from the restroom, Maggie invites her to join them. Owen gets an empty chair from another table and pulls it up for Nell. She thanks Owen and settles into her chair.*

Nell: Phew! I'm so glad to be here. I apologize for being late. I went to the wrong Java House!

Maggie: Oh no, I'm so sorry! I didn't even think about the *other* Java House! I never go to that one. Oh gosh. I'm sorry about that.

Nell: No problem at all, dear. I enjoyed my cup of coffee on the way over. I hope I didn't disrupt your conversation.

Narrator: *For a moment, no one says anything.*

Maggie: Well, we were talking about...frustration and disappointment.

Nell: Oh?

Melvin: Yes.

Narrator: *It is quiet for a few more moments.*

Nell: Hmmm. Those are tough emotions. How do you deal with feelings like frustration and disappointment?

Josie: I talk to someone I trust.

Nell: Brilliant. Personally, I take some deep breaths when I feel frustrated. If I can, I close my eyes and repeat a mantra, which is an encouraging phrase we repeat silently to ourselves. My current mantra is, "Peace is a choice."

Owen: That's a pretty good one.

Nell: I also know how it feels to be disappointed. This may sound silly, but disappointment makes me think of a bee sting. Disappointment feels like a sharp, stinging pain to me.

Narrator: *Tia nods her head.*

Tia: It was my disappointment we were talking about. I have a DJ business called Tia's Tunes. I didn't get a job I really wanted.

Nell: I'm sorry. You must be Tia?

Narrator: *Tia nods her head again.*

Nell: I'm sorry, Tia.

Tia: Thank you.

Maggie: Oh gosh, we haven't introduced ourselves yet! How about we go around the table and tell Nell our names?

Narrator: *Steve is sitting next to Tia. He introduces himself and the others follow.*

Nell: It's lovely to meet you all. I understand you are readers *and* writers?

Melvin: That's right. We can do it all.

Nell: Brilliant. What do you all think about writing a short story together?

Josie: Sure. When?

Nell: Right now, I was thinking. Is that all right?

Josie: Fine with me. Everyone?

Narrator: *Josie looks at the others, who nod their heads.*

Nell: Brilliant. What if I get us started with a scenario, and then we go around the table, each person adding one sentence to the story as we go. We'll go around several times and see where we end up. How does that sound?

Melvin: I don't understand.

Owen: Remember, Mel, when we wrote that story about the hot air balloon ride?

Narrator: *Melvin nods his head.*

Owen: It's like that. We went around the table and added our own ideas, one at a time.

Melvin: Okay, got it.

Steve: Are we going to write the story down or just say it out loud?

Nell: That's up to you all.

Josie: Can we say it out loud? I didn't bring any of my writing supplies tonight.

Nell: Sure! Brilliant. Okay, here goes...

Act III, Scene II

Narrator: *Nell clears her throat and closes her eyes. After a few moments, she begins the story.*

Nell: It could be a once in a lifetime chance. Jenny had already won front row tickets to see her favorite band...um...can someone give me the name of a band?

Maggie: How about Owen and the Readers?

Narrator: *Maggie winks at Owen, since he shared earlier that he had been in a band.*

Nell: Brilliant! Okay... It could be a once in a lifetime chance. Jenny had already won front row tickets to see her favorite band, Owen and the Readers. She and her friends were having so much fun at the concert, singing and cheering. Just before the concert ended, a man with a mustache and at least six badges around his neck walked up to Jenny and her friends. He said, "Hello, ladies. I'm Joe. I'm with the band.

We usually invite some of our best fans backstage after concerts to meet the band. Are you interested?"

Jenny's friends said, "Yes!" and, "Of course!" But Jenny didn't say anything. The thought of meeting Owen and the Readers all of a sudden made her feel like she might faint.

Narrator: *Nell looks to her right, where Owen is sitting.*

Nell: All right, Owen, is it?

Narrator: *Owen nods his head.*

Nell: Owen, now it's your turn to add one sentence to the story. You can say whatever you like, but how about we agree to keep the story about Jenny and the concert. Sound good, everyone?

Narrator: *Everyone nods their heads.*

Owen: Okay, my turn?

Nell: Yes. We meet Jenny and her friends after they've been invited to meet the band.

Owen: Jenny had always wanted to meet Owen and the Readers...

Narrator: *Owen blushes a little when he says* Owen and the Readers.

Owen: ...but now she felt scared.

Narrator: *Owen looks to his right where Eddie is sitting. The book club members continue to build the story by going around the table and adding one sentence at a time.*

Eddie: After all, Owen and the Readers was the most popular band in the country.

Melvin: Owen and the Readers rock!

Emma: Jenny was nervous to meet the band.

Josie: She was afraid she would say the wrong thing or embarrass herself in front of them.

Steve: Then she thought, *I only live once, so I should give it a try.*

Tia: Jenny tells her friends she will do it. Her friends cheer.

Josie: Wait, Tia. Only one sentence at a time.

Nell: I think that's fine. Her friends probably would cheer.

Maggie: When the concert ends, Joe walks back over to Jenny and her friends.

Nell: He says, "Okay, ladies. Please follow me closely because there are a lot of people backstage."

Owen: Jenny couldn't believe how many people were backstage.

Eddie: All those people only made her feel more nervous.

Melvin: Jenny wished she had her magic wand.

Steve: A magic wand? What does a magic wand have to do with a concert?

Nell: I don't think we know yet. Let's keep going. This is brilliant.

Emma: Jenny wanted her magic wand to make all the people disappear.

Josie: But Jenny did not have her magic wand.

Steve: Because who brings a magic wand to a concert?

Josie: That's not a complete sentence.

Steve: Okay... They wouldn't let magic wands backstage anyway.

Tia: Then they reached a door with a big gold star on it.

Maggie: Jenny knew that must be the band's private room.

Nell: Jenny's belly flipped, but she was starting to feel more excited than nervous.

Owen: Joe knocked on the door and opened it.

Eddie: When they looked in the room, it was empty!

Melvin: The band was gone!

Emma: Jenny and her friends were confused.

Josie: Joe asked them to wait while he went to find the band.

Steve: When he returned, he told them that the band was already on the bus.

Tia: Jenny felt disappointed and relieved at the same time.

Maggie: One of Jenny's friends asked Joe if there was any way they could see the tour bus.

Nell: Joe said, "I suppose there's no harm in that."

Owen: So they went to see the tour bus.

Eddie: All of a sudden, from across the parking lot, they saw the bus door open.

Melvin: The band got off the bus.

Emma: Jenny and her friends were so surprised!

Josie: Joe walked over to the band and asked them why they got off the bus.

Steve: The bus driver said the bus wouldn't start.

Tia: The band noticed Jenny and her friends standing there.

Maggie: Joe asked the band if they would meet with Jenny and her friends, and the next thing Jenny knew, they were walking toward the most famous band in the land.

Nell: Jenny thought she might throw up on that short walk.

Owen: She felt woozy and dizzy and very nervous.

Eddie: Jenny knew that throwing up in front of her favorite band would, you know, ruin the moment.

Melvin: But she barfed anyway!

Narrator: *Melvin, Owen, Emma, Tia, and Eddie laugh out loud. Maggie starts laughing because her friends are laughing. Then, Maggie's goofy laugh makes everyone, including Nell, laugh. Finally the laughter quiets down.*

Emma: Nell, do you like Nancy Drew?

Nell: Certainly. Are you a fan?

Emma: I've read all the books.

Nell: Brilliant!

Steve: Wait. Aren't we going to finish the story?

Josie: That's right. We stopped going around the table after Melvin told us that Jenny barfed.

Melvin: You're welcome, everyone.

Narrator: *Melvin smirks and Owen and Eddie laugh.*

Nell: Sure, why not finish the story?

Maggie: All right, Emma. You have a tough act to follow. What do you want to say after "she barfed anyway"?

Emma: She was embarrassed but nobody laughed at her.

Josie: Her friends comforted her.

Steve: They gave her mints, tissues, and hand sanitizer.

Tia: They met the band and everyone was super cool about Jenny getting sick.

Maggie: Jenny's favorite part was learning that the lead singer Owen had once fainted in front of the band U2. The end.

Nell: Well, that worked out quite nicely, didn't it?

Melvin: Like I said, we can do it all.

What Do You Think?

1.   Have you ever had such a good laugh that your body felt better afterward?

2.   Tia thinks she wasn't chosen as the wedding DJ because of the way her cerebral palsy affects her speech. Have you ever had someone turn you down for something because you have a disability? What did that feel like?

3.   Do you have a favorite band or musician?

4.   If you had to choose a mantra for yourself, what would it be?

Play 6

Party People

CHARACTERS

Emma

Tia

Nina

Owen

Keith

Fawn

Melvin

Josie

Eddie

Steve

Cheryl

Zane

Nash

Narrator

Act I

Narrator: *Emma and Josie are hosting a New Year's Eve party in their apartment, and they have invited their friends from book club as well as a few other people. Josie is especially excited for Steve to arrive since they got back together just before Christmas. The apartment is decorated in gold and silver with balloons, signs, and streamers. Next to the front door, there is a bowl of noise makers and party hats for everyone. Emma and Josie are dressed in fancier clothes than they usually wear to book club. They are filling bowls and platters on their dining room table with food such as potato skins, chicken wings, veggies and hummus, and much more. There is a knock on the door.*

Emma: That must be Tia. She was going to come early to set up her DJ equipment.

Josie: My hands are covered in chip dip. Can you let her in?

Emma: Sure. Coming, Tia!

Narrator: *Emma opens the door. Tia and her father are there, surrounded by several pieces of electronic equipment.*

Emma: Tia! I'm so glad you're here!

Tia: Me too! My dad is going to help me carry in all this equipment, and then he's going home.

Narrator: *Tia's dad salutes his daughter to show that he is following her orders. He picks up two large speakers.*

Emma: We thought we could put the music in front of the fireplace. What do you think?

Tia: Good choice. If you could help me carry in the rest of these things, I'll get set up and the party can begin!

Narrator: *Emma, Tia, and Tia's dad place the equipment on the floor in front of the fireplace. Tia thanks her father and gives him a hug. He wishes the women a happy New Year and tells Tia that he will be back to pick her up at 1:00 a.m.*

Josie: Hi, Tia!

Tia: Hi, Josie! I'm so excited for tonight! I put together an awesome playlist.

Josie: Great! Do you need any help setting up?

Tia: No, thanks. This place looks amazing, by the way!

Emma: Thanks! We've been decorating all day!

Josie: The food is almost ready if you're hungry, Tia.

Tia: I'm not hungry, but could I have a glass of water or whatever you have to drink?

Josie: The punch! Emma, we almost forgot the punch!

Emma: Oh my gosh, we did!

Josie: I'll go make it. First, let me get you a glass of water, Tia.

Narrator: *Josie pours a glass of water and hands it to Tia. There is a knock at the door.*

Emma: I'll get it!

Narrator: *When Emma opens the door, Eddie and his wife Nina are there.*

Emma: Yay! Happy New Year! Come in.

Narrator: *Eddie and Nina walk inside. Emma hugs them and shows them the party hats and noise makers.*

Eddie: Tia! I'm pumped to hear "Tia's Tunes"!

Narrator: *Eddie gestures at Tia's DJ booth, which she is setting up. In the front is a sign with sparkly, colorful letters that says "Tia's Tunes."*

Tia: Eddie! Nina! *Feliz año Nuevo*!

Eddie *and* **Nina**: Feliz año Nuevo!

Narrator: *Josie returns from the kitchen.*

Josie: Hi, guys. Happy New Year!

Eddie: Happy New Year to you, too, Josie!

Nina: It's so nice to see you again, Josie. Your apartment looks amazing!

Josie: Thank you! Emma and I worked hard on it. Also, I just made the world's best punch. One bowl has champagne in it and the other is non-alcoholic.

Emma: We should probably make signs so people know which is which.

Narrator: *Josie raises two small signs to show Emma. One says "Has Alcohol" and the other says "Does NOT Have Alcohol."*

Nina: You ladies have thought of everything!

Emma: I'm going to get a glass of punch with champagne. Do you want one, Nina?

Nina: No, thanks. You go ahead.

Narrator: *Tia's music starts playing at a low volume so everyone can talk to each other without shouting.*

Emma pours herself a large glass of punch, and Josie returns to the kitchen. A moment later, there is another knock on the door.

Eddie: I'll get it!

Narrator: *Eddie opens the door. Steve is there.*

Eddie: Steve! Good to see you, man!

Steve: Good to see you, too.

Tia: Hi, Steve! Come in!

Narrator: *Steve walks into the living room. He says hi to Tia, Emma, and Nina. He keeps walking through the apartment until he finds Josie in the kitchen.*

Steve: Hi. You look very nice.

Josie: Oh hi! Thanks, you look nice, too. Will you hand me the oven mitt on the counter next to you?

Narrator: *Josie points to a red oven mitt. Steve hands it to her. She opens the oven door and pulls out a tray of stuffed mushrooms.*

Josie: You look so nice in that shirt. I knew it would be a good color for you.

Steve: My parents teased me for wearing it tonight.

Josie: Why? That's such a nice shirt!

Steve: They know you bought it for me. My mom said you probably told me exactly what to wear tonight.

Josie: Your parents don't like me, do they?

Steve: Um, not exactly. But I shouldn't have said anything. Ugh.

Josie: It's too late now. Why don't your parents like me? What did I do?

Steve: It's because of how things were when we dated before. You know, you were kinda bossy. They didn't like it.

Josie: But, but that was back then!

Steve: I know. My parents don't know what they're talking about.

Josie: Did you tell them that?

Steve: No! Ugh! I didn't say anything. They have strong opinions, you know. I didn't want to get into a fight right before the party.

Josie: I guess I understand. This hurts my feelings, though.

Steve: I'm sorry. I don't want to hurt your feelings.

Narrator: *Steve reaches out his arms for a hug, but Josie waits.*

Josie: Are *you* happy we're back together?

Steve: Yes! I'm really happy we're back together.

Josie: I guess that's the most important thing...for tonight. You have to talk to your parents, Steve. I mean, I'm not telling you what to do, but this isn't fair.

Steve: I know. I'll talk to them soon.

Josie: How soon?

Steve: How about tomorrow?

Narrator: *Josie nods her head and the couple hugs.*

Josie: Good. Thank you. Will you help me carry these plates out to the table?

Narrator: *Steve and Josie carry plates of food to the dining room table. Nina, Emma, and Eddie are on the couch. Tia is looking through her playlist and moving her head to the beat of the music.*

Nina: Emma, how have you been? I was so sad to miss you this Christmas. I get all the crummy shifts since I'm one of the newest nurses at the hospital.

Emma: I missed you, too. And now I miss Maggie. I wish she was here.

Nina: I wish she was here, too. You know how she looks forward to this vacation every year. She has so many friends in Mexico now!

Emma: We could call her later.

Eddie: Or we could call her now...

Emma: Yes! Let's call her.

Nina: Well, before we do that, Eddie and I have some news to share with you.

Emma: Okay.

Narrator: *Eddie and Nina look at each other in a strange way, and this makes Emma nervous and confused.*

Nina: Emma, how do you feel about being an aunt?

Emma: That would be the best. I would love to be— wait a minute! Are you having a baby?

Nina: We are.

Narrator: *Emma screams so loudly that Josie and Steve run out of the kitchen to find out what is happening. Tia stops the music.*

Emma: Guess what!?

Josie: What? Are you okay?

Emma: I'm going to be an aunt!

Narrator: *Emma does a "happy dance" while Tia, Josie, and Steve congratulate Nina and Eddie.*

Emma: Let's call Maggie and tell her!

Eddie: All right, let's do it...

Narrator: *Eddie dials Maggie's phone and uses his speakerphone so everyone in the room can hear.*

Maggie answers the phone, but before Eddie and Nina can say anything, Emma screams, "We're going to be aunts, Maggie! They're having a baby!" Maggie screams just like Emma did. The family talks for a couple minutes, then Maggie wishes everyone a Happy New Year. They hang up and Eddie looks at Emma.

<u>Eddie</u>: Emma, it's possible you might be as excited as Nina and I are!

Emma: I'm SO excited! When will the baby be here?

Nina: The baby is due in June. I made Eddie wait to tell you because I wanted to be here when you found out. I'm so glad I did!

Narrator: *Nina and Emma continue to talk. Eventually, the subject changes to a new co-worker at the rec center where Emma works.*

Emma: His name is Charlie, and he's really nice and really funny. I invited him to the party tonight, but he already had plans.

Nina: Bummer. Maybe I'll get to meet him another time.

Emma: Josie invited one of her co-workers, too. Hey, Josie! When do you think your friend from work will be here?

Josie: I don't know. Owen and Melvin aren't here yet either. But I guess that's okay. People don't have to be right on time for a party.

Narrator: *There is another knock on the door. When Eddie opens it, Owen and a woman in a leather jacket walk in. The book club members recognize the woman from Java House.*

Eddie: Owen!

Owen: Eddie! Hi everybody! You all know Cheryl, right?

Emma: Sure! You work at Java House.

Cheryl: That's right. Thanks for having me! Everything looks so nice.

Emma: Thank you! There is *a lot* of food in the dining room. Please help yourself!

Narrator: *Owen looks for Melvin, but doesn't see him.*

Owen: Hey, is Melvin here?

Steve: No, he's not. That's odd. Melvin is usually early.

Owen: I'll text him.

Narrator: *Owen texts Melvin. Tia turns up the music. Josie dims the lights.*

Eddie: I'm feeling the party vibe. You better watch out or I might start dancing!

Owen: Oh, I'd like to see that!

Narrator: *Eddie's dance moves are interrupted by very loud knocking on the door. Josie answers it, and her eyes open wide when she sees a group of five people on the porch. They appear to be drunk, and they are dressed up for a much fancier party than Josie and Emma's.*

Act II

Narrator: *Josie spots her co-worker Keith in the group and invites them inside.*

Josie: Hey, Keith.

Keith: Hey, lady! Thanks for inviting us to your party! I hope you don't mind that I brought a few friends with me.

Narrator: *Josie* does *mind. Each person was invited to bring* one *guest. Not four guests. Josie wants to be a good host, though, so she welcomes them. She introduces Keith to the others in the room. Keith introduces his friends: Zane, Zoe, Fawn, and Nash.*

Josie: Come on in, everybody. Help yourself to food and punch.

Fawn: Thanks!

Narrator: *Fawn grabs a couple noise makers from the basket by the door and gives one to Keith. As they blow the noise makers, Nash's phone rings. He answers it with a shout, "Happy New Year!" Zane pulls a flask from his jacket pocket and takes a big drink. Then there is another knock at the door. Fawn opens the door while blowing her noise maker. Melvin is there.*

Melvin: Is this Josie and Emma's apartment?

Narrator: *Emma walks over to greet Melvin. Fawn joins her friends, who have found the punchbowl.*

Emma: Hi, Melvin. I'm surprised you came so late! Did something happen?

Melvin: I had new staff tonight. Gil is off work. The new person was late picking me up.

Emma: That's not good.

Melvin: I know. I was upset. I hate to be late! The new guy said he got lost on the way to my house.

Emma: Oh. Did you tell him you were upset?

Melvin: I did. He said he was sorry, and I accepted his apology. I don't want to be upset at the New Year's Eve party.

Emma: Well, I'm glad you're here. Do you want snacks or punch? You should try the punch. It's so good.

Melvin: Okay, I will. Who are all these people?

Narrator: *Just then, Owen and Cheryl walk over to greet Melvin. Emma excuses herself to refill her cup of punch.*

Owen: Melvin! Glad you're here, man.

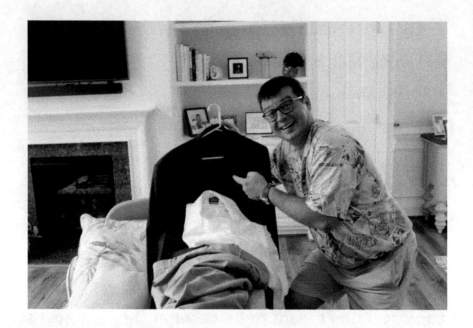

<u>Melvin</u>: I had new staff tonight. He was twenty-three minutes late picking me up! I was not happy. But it won't ruin my night. It's New Year's Eve, and...

<u>Narrator</u>: *Melvin clears his throat.*

<u>Melvin</u>: I have a new outfit.

<u>Narrator</u>: *Melvin smiles, bows his head, and waves his arm in front of his stylish new jacket, shirt, and slacks.*

<u>Cheryl</u>: Hey, I was gonna tell you you're looking spiffy, my friend.

Melvin: Thank you!

Narrator: *Cheryl and Melvin give each other a fist bump. Keith, Fawn, and Nash cheer on Zoe as she drinks a whole glass of punch in one gulp.*

Melvin: Who are all these people?

Owen: One of them is Josie's friend from Big Jim's Barbecue. The others are his friends, I guess. They got a head start on the party, I can tell.

Cheryl: For sure. Seems like they're having fun, huh? I don't miss my drinking days, though. *Nobody* misses my drinking days!

Narrator: *Cheryl and Owen chuckle.*

Melvin: They shouldn't drive if they're drinking.

Owen: Right. Hopefully they took a cab or rideshare.

Narrator: *Nash finally finishes his phone call and shouts to no one in particular.*

Nash: All right, party people!

Narrator: *Owen and Cheryl reply, "Woohoo!"*

Cheryl: Hey, I'm going to go talk to Tia about my friend's fiftieth birthday party in the spring. She just told me she wants to hire a DJ. I'm gonna go hook them up.

Owen: That's a wonderful idea.

Narrator: *Cheryl smiles at Owen, then walks over to the DJ booth to talk to Tia. Melvin turns to Owen.*

Melvin: Do you want to get some food? I smell bacon over there.

Owen: Let's do it. Hey, man, you gotta see Cheryl's car...

Narrator: *Owen and Melvin walk to the dining room. At the DJ booth, Cheryl tells Tia about her friend's birthday party. Tia is excited about possibly getting the gig. She gives Cheryl a new business card.*

Cheryl: I hope it works out. Owen said it was a wonderful idea!

Tia: Hey, I didn't know you and Owen were hanging out! Wait—you *are* dating, right?

Cheryl: Yeah, I guess we are.

Tia: How did it happen, if you don't mind me asking?

Cheryl: Sure, I don't mind. It started one day at Java House when I was wearing an old Rolling Stones T-shirt. Owen asked if I'd ever seen The Stones. It turns out we were at the same Stones concert in 1996! We started talking about music and concerts and then all sorts of things. The past few months he's been walking to Java House to meet me on my breaks. You wouldn't believe how much we have in common.

Tia: Like what?

Cheryl: Well, there's music and concerts. We both take our coffee with one sugar, no cream. Plus, neither of us drinks alcohol anymore. Also, I drive an old Mustang that Owen loves. Sometimes I think he likes my car more than me!

Tia: I'm happy for you both. Owen is one of the best guys I know.

Narrator: *Cheryl looks over at Owen and smiles.*

Cheryl: He is pretty great. It looks like he and Melvin are enjoying the food. Melvin's got a tower of potato skins! I think I'll join them. Can I bring you anything?

Tia: No, thanks. I'm about to turn this party up a notch.

Cheryl: Cool. Well, party on!

Narrator: *Cheryl joins Owen and Melvin at the food table. Nearby at the punchbowl, Emma pours herself another glass and looks around at all the people. Keith and his friends are gathered by the DJ booth to sing along to the song Tia just started. Melvin puts down his plate to join the group of singers. Owen and Cheryl are happily filling plates with food. Steve and Nina are playing a card game on the coffee table. Josie is next to the DJ booth, talking with Tia.*

Emma has never hosted so many people. She feels proud and happy. Just then, Eddie joins her at the punchbowl.

Eddie: Hey, sis. What do you think of this party?

Emma: It's the best. I'm so happy.

Eddie: You sure that isn't the punch talking?

Emma: What?

Eddie: I think you've had a lot of punch, sis.

Emma: Well, it's delicious. Besides, don't worry about me. This is my last glass, and it's not—

Eddie: Not my business?

Emma: Right.

Eddie: Okay, got it. I actually came over here to tell you what a great party this is.

Emma: I know! Josie and I are good at hosting. And I love decorating! I want to stay here. I mean, I want to live on my own, not with you or Maggie.

Narrator: *Eddie smiles at his sister and nods his head.*

Emma: I don't want to hurt your feelings, though.

Eddie: Don't worry about me and Maggie. We'll be fine. I can tell you're happy, Em, and that makes me happy.

Emma: Thanks, Eddie. You don't think Maggie will be sad?

Eddie: She might be sad at first. She'll be okay, though. She wants you to be happy, just like I do.

Emma: I'm going to be an aunt!

Eddie: That's right! Can you believe *I'm* going to be a dad?

Narrator: *Emma just shakes her head no. She and Eddie crack up laughing. For the next few minutes, they watch all the partiers having a great time. Cheryl and Owen have joined the group in front of the DJ booth. Melvin and Keith have a dance-off, and the group cheers for both. Fawn continues to blow her noise maker. As the song changes, Zane and Nash head to the dining room. Instead of getting plates of food, they decide to toss cashews into each other's mouths. As Zane leans to catch the next cashew in his mouth, he bumps into the table and Josie's water pitcher falls over and breaks. At the sound of breaking glass, Zoe, Fawn, and Nash whoop and laugh. Zane bends down to pick up some of the broken glass. Josie and others rush over to see what happened.*

Josie: Are you okay? What happened? Stop! You're bleeding!

Narrator: *Zane looks at his finger and sees that he has cut himself while trying to pick up pieces of the broken water pitcher. At the sight of his own blood, he faints and knocks a clock off the wall as he falls to the floor.*

Act III

Narrator: *Several people scream as Zane falls. Nina asks Emma to go get first aid supplies and then asks everyone to back away. Zane wakes up after a few moments, and Nina bandages the cut on his finger.*

Nina: Did you hit your head?

Zane: When?

Nina: Just now, when you passed out.

Zane: I don't think so. I just can't handle the sight of my own blood.

Emma: Is he okay, Nina?

Nina: I think so, but I don't think it's safe for you to drink any more alcohol tonight.

Narrator: *Zane looks up at his friends. Zoe gestures that they should leave the party by pointing her thumb toward the door. Fawn and Nash nod their heads.*

Nash: We're going to head out.

Party People

Fawn: Thank you so much for having us, Emma and Jodie!

Josie: It's *Josie*.

Fawn: Sorry, Josie. Our driver is waiting for us outside, so we have to go.

Nina: Good.

Narrator*: Several people laugh.*

Nina: I mean, it's good that none of you are driving.

Narrator*: Zoe and Nash help Zane stand up. The group walks to the front door and they wait for Keith, who has started to soak up the spilled water with little cocktail napkins.*

Keith: Shoot. I'm sorry, Josie. We broke your water pitcher and made such a mess.

Josie: It's fine. You better go. Your party bus is leaving.

Keith: I feel bad. Are you sure?

Narrator*: Josie nods her head yes and gives Keith a quick smile, even though she is annoyed.*

Keith: Okay. Gosh, great party, everyone! Thanks so much. I'll see you at work, Josie!

Josie: I'll see you at work.

Narrator: *Keith and his friends make as much noise leaving the party as they did when they arrived. Steve begins to soak up the spilled water with a kitchen towel. He wrings it out in the sink and uses it to wipe the broken glass off the table and into the trash can. Eddie finds a broom and sweeps the glass on the floor into a dustpan.*

Josie: Thanks for cleaning up, guys.

Eddie: You're welcome.

Steve: I'm glad they're gone.

Josie: So am I! I have some things to say to Keith when I see him at work.

Eddie: I bet you do!

Steve: Josie, do you want to go relax on the couch for a few minutes?

Josie: That sounds nice.

Narrator: *Josie takes Steve's hand. They walk to the couch and sit down. Josie leans over and gives Steve a kiss on the cheek. Steve turns his head and they kiss briefly on the lips. Nina checks her watch and looks at Eddie.*

Nina: Eddie, are you ready to go home? I don't know if I can make it to midnight.

Eddie: Every party has a pooper, that's why we invited you…

Eddie *and* **Emma**: Party pooper, party pooper!

Melvin: Hey, I know that song!

Nina: Very funny.

Emma: Can't you stay till midnight?

Eddie: Sorry, Em. Nina and I go to bed early these days.

Nina: You wouldn't believe how tired I get since I got pregnant.

Eddie: It's true. Nina used to be a night owl. She's in bed by 9:00 p.m. now!

Nina: Emma and Josie, this was a fabulous party. Happy New Year, everyone!

Eddie: Yeah, awesome job, sis. Awesome job, Josie.

Narrator: *Josie says, "Thanks." Emma hugs Eddie and Nina. Then they say "Goodbye" and "Happy New Year" to everyone else and leave the party.*

Cheryl: Well, they're going to miss the main event!

Melvin: The main event?

Cheryl: The countdown to midnight. That's the best part of New Year's Eve!

Narrator: *Owen looks at his watch and shakes his head.*

Cheryl: What?

Owen: I might need some coffee. It's only 10:15.

Cheryl: Oh, coffee sounds good. Do you have any here?

Emma: We have coffee. It's not Java House coffee, though.

Cheryl: Whatever you have will be great.

Narrator: *Over the next hour and forty minutes, the friends talk about the events of the evening so far. They laugh and laugh. Some have coffee. Some have punch. Melvin treats the group to a five-minute stand-up comedy set and is excited about how many of his jokes made his friends laugh. Tia takes music requests from the crowd. Emma and Melvin and Cheryl dance sometimes, but Josie, Steve, and Owen do not dance. They play games and go back for another round of food. At 11:55, Tia turns the music down very low.*

Tia: Hey, everybody! I want to make a New Year's toast. Then I'll stop talking so we can turn on the TV to watch the ball drop in Times Square. Grab whatever you're drinking and hold it up.

Narrator: *Tia gives everyone time to grab their drinks. Josie doesn't have any punch left in her glass. Steve offers to refill her glass. She accepts his offer; however, Steve finds the punchbowls empty.*

Steve: What else would you like to drink?

Josie: Do we have any ginger ale left?

Steve: None in the fridge; I'll check the back porch.

Narrator: *Seconds seem to take minutes. It is now 11:57. Steve returns and tells Josie there is no ginger ale outside.*

Steve: What else would you like?

Josie: Water will be fine, thanks.

Narrator: *Steve struggles to find a clean glass for Josie's water. Melvin looks at his watch. It is 11:58.*

Steve: Josie, will a coffee mug be okay?

Melvin: Yes! A coffee mug is fine. But *this year*, please! We only have two minutes left, man!

Narrator: *The friends burst out laughing and tell Steve to hurry. Steve brings Josie a mug of cold water. Tia holds up her glass and everyone follows.*

Tia: Happy New Year, everyone! A toast to the year we leave behind. We read five books, had a yard sale, picked apples, and even got stuck on an elevator!

Narrator: *Everyone laughs.*

Tia: And a toast to the year ahead! *Salud*! Cheers!

Narrator: *The friends clink their glasses against one another's. Quickly, Tia pauses the background music. Josie turns on the TV and changes to the channel where they show the ball drop in New York City's Times Square. Excitement builds in the room until the countdown arrives.*

Tia, **Emma**, **Josie**, **Steve**, **Melvin**, **Owen** and **Cheryl**: Ten! Nine! Eight! Seven! Six! Five! Four! Three! Two! One! Happy New Year!

What Do You Think?

1. Have you ever hosted a party before? What was it like? Do you like energetic dance parties or quiet get-togethers?

2. Josie finds out that Steve's parents don't like her. What do you think that would feel like? What should Steve do?

3. Are you an aunt or uncle? How many nieces or nephews do you have? What does it feel like to be an aunt or uncle?

4. Josie says she has some things to say to Keith when she sees him at work. What do you think she will say to him?

An Update
from Owen

HI, IT'S OWEN. I hope you enjoyed reading about our Next Chapter Book Club! I want to let you know about some changes that have happened since our New Year's Eve party. There's a virus called COVID-19 (some people call it "coronavirus") in our world right now. COVID-19 is a very contagious virus, which means it's easy for people to pass it to others. Some people who get the virus don't even know they have it! But other people who get the virus might get very sick. Some people even die. Melvin's Uncle Stan got the virus and had to go into the hospital. We were all worried, but thankfully, Uncle Stan got better!

It has been a strange and scary time for everyone. Since it is so easy to spread the virus, we had to make some big changes to our book club meetings. The biggest change is that we can't meet at Java House right now. It even closed for two months, which was really hard for my girlfriend Cheryl because she works there. Thankfully, the drive-thru window reopened, so she has gone back to work. Cheryl says people come through the drive-thru all day long. I guess people still need their coffee!

An Update from Owen

Since we can't meet at Java House right now, our book club has been meeting on our computers. It's different, but kind of cool! At first, I couldn't join the group because I didn't have a computer or the right kind of phone. Then, Eddie and his wife Nina gave me a computer they don't use anymore. It was really nice of them. I have a new bill each month for internet service, but it's worth it. There is so much to do on the computer! The best thing is seeing my friends from book club on Wednesday nights. I think we look like the beginning of the *Brady Bunch* TV show on the computer screen. Just like in our book club meetings at Java House, we take turns reading one page at a time. We talk about the book and about what's going on in each other's lives.

As for what is going on in *my* life, I'm happy to say that things are going great with Cheryl.

She started spending more time at my apartment when Java House closed. I really like it when she comes over. Thankfully, the hardware store where I work has stayed open. I'm not sure how I would pay my bills if the store closed. We have to wear masks all the time at work now, and sometimes it makes me hot. Also, we ask our customers to wear masks, so at least we're all hot together.

Keeping a mask on isn't easy for everyone. When Steve's warehouse reopened, they also had to wear masks. Steve said it made him feel like he couldn't breathe. He tried different kinds of masks, but he had a hard time with all of them. Finally, his parents found a special kind of hat he could wear to work. He wore it one night during a book club meeting. It has a clear plastic shield that hangs down from the bill of the hat. Steve doesn't like wearing the hat either, but at least he can go to work and stay safe.

Josie said her job at Big Jim's is different, too.

She also wears a mask, and says they can only seat customers at every other table. This is because of something called "social distancing," which means keeping at least six feet between yourself and other people. Josie is really good at following rules. She said she helps one of the other hostesses figure out where to seat people. That sounds like Josie!

Emma said they are wearing masks and social distancing at the rec center where she works, too. She can only let a few people at a time into the gym to work out. Also, she has had fewer shifts than she used to. She decided to use the extra time to learn a new hobby called cross-stitching. She's really good at it! You should see some of the things she's made. For Maggie's birthday last month, Emma stitched two young girls holding hands, like she and Maggie used to do when they were young. Emma said Maggie cried when she opened it. It must have meant a lot to her.

Since Melvin doesn't have a job, he and his parents have spent a lot of time doing puzzles and watching movies at home. He was getting pretty bored until he found out he could watch as much stand-up comedy as he wants on the internet. Now, Melvin says his parents have to ask him to share the family computer!

Of course, Tia's DJ business has been very slow. But last week, she shared some great news with us. Tia's Tunes will be the DJ for a wedding next year! Tia has wanted this for a long time, so she was really excited. We all cheered for her, and Emma surprised us by blowing on a noisemaker that was left over from the New Year's Eve party. That made everyone laugh!

We're all looking forward to going back to Java House when it is safe. In the meantime, we're doing what we can to stay safe and healthy. And on Wednesday nights, you can find us all in front of our computer screens, reading, talking, and laughing as usual.

About the Authors

JILLIAN OBER is Program Manager at The Ohio State University Nisonger Center, where she has worked since 2004 to promote community inclusion and social connections for people with disabilities. Among the programs Jillian manages is Next Chapter Book Club, a widely successful, community-based book club program for people with intellectual and developmental disabilities. Jillian received both her undergraduate and graduate degrees from The Ohio State University. She is a very proud aunt, animal lover, and wannabe interior designer with way too many decorative pillows.

DR. TOM FISH is the founder of the Next Chapter Book Club program and worked many years at The Ohio State University Nisonger Center on Disabilities. He is passionate about helping individuals with disabilities and their families find worth, support, and value in their lives. Tom now lives in Wilmington, North Carolina, where he is close to his amazing family and grand dogs. He loves spending time with his longtime partner Lyna and works sort of hard at improving his skills on the ukulele.

CPSIA information can be obtained
at www.ICGtesting.com
Printed in the USA
LVHW081416150321
681597LV00027B/209